ENGAGED TO A FRIEND

CONVENIENT ARRANGEMENTS (BOOK 6)

ROSE PEARSON

ENGAGED TO A FRIEND

Convenient Arrangements

(Book 6)

By

Rose Pearson

ENGAGED TO A FRIEND

PROLOGUE

"It is certainly a pleasure to be back in London!"

Looking out of the carriage window, Tabitha let out a long sigh of contentment. "Indeed it is," she said, smiling to herself. "Whilst I will not pretend that the past few months have been uneventful, for they have been most engaging, there is certainly a fresh excitement in coming back for the Season."

Lady Dinah Ashbrook laughed as the carriage began to slow. "I am very glad to have you returned also," she said, as Tabitha smiled back at her. "You know very well that my husband is one of the dullest gentlemen in all of England!"

Knowing Lady Dinah was teasing, Tabitha laughed softly and shook her head. "If I know Lord Ashbrook at all, then I am certain that he will have already planned a great many events for you to not only attend but also to host!"

"Indeed, he has," Lady Ashbrook replied with a fond

smile spreading across her face as she thought of her husband. "I confess that I am very much looking forward to this Season." The carriage came to a stop, and the door was pulled open, ready for them to depart. "Which is precisely why I *must* have a few new things!"

Tabitha stepped out into the London street and inhaled a deep breath, a familiar delight spreading through her chest as she took in the scene surrounding her. London was a most welcome place, for it meant that she could enjoy the many exciting entertainments that it had to offer and would be able to see and converse with her many friends and acquaintances. Being a widow meant a great deal of liberty and, whilst Tabitha had been sorrowful over her husband's death some three years ago, she had soon taken hold of her new freedom with great satisfaction.

"It is quite wonderful," she agreed as Lady Ashbrook began to hurry across the pavement towards a few of the shops. "Now, what precisely are you seeking this afternoon, Lady Ashbrook?"

Lady Ashbrook glanced back over her shoulder and then, with a small shrug, allowed herself a quiet laugh. "I am not quite certain," she declared. "My dear husband has told me I should purchase whatever I require, whatever I wish, and I cannot disoblige him!"

"That is true enough!" Tabitha laughed, coming over towards her friend and looking at the bonnets sitting proudly in the window. "A new bonnet, mayhap?"

Lady Ashbrook's eyes twinkled. "Mayhap indeed," she laughed, going to the door. "Shall we, Lady Croome?"

With a smile, Tabitha entered the shop alongside her friend and began to peruse the items there. This was the beginning of her Season, and Tabitha could not help but feel very contented indeed.

"Lady Croome."

Turning swiftly, Tabitha recognized the imposing figure of Lady Pellingham. She was a well-known lady amongst the *beau monde*, having married the Marquess of Pellingham around a decade ago and, since then, providing him with not only the heir and the spare but three other very robust children.

"Good afternoon, Lady Pellingham," she said quickly, curtsying. "How very good to see you again." It would not do to fall out of favor with Lady Pellingham, given that she had the power to remove practically anyone from their position within society, should she wish to do so. "I do hope you are well?"

"Very well," Lady Pellingham replied, a slight air of arrogance floating about her. "This is now your third Season in London, is it not?"

Tabitha let a frown flicker across her brow. "My third Season?" she repeated, wondering what the lady meant.

"Since you returned to the fray," Lady Pellingham said, looking down her sharp nose at Tabitha, her dark blue eyes a little narrowed. "It has been four years since you buried your husband."

Quickly coming to an understanding of what the lady meant, Tabitha gave her a small smile. "Yes, indeed," she said, recalling how, at the tender age of sixteen, she had been not only engaged but wed to Viscount Croome. A year and a half later, he had passed away. It had been entirely his own foolishness that had brought about his demise, for he had been something of a wastrel who drank to excess whenever he could. Trying to ride one's horse when one was fully in one's cups was a foolish endeavor, and it had left Tabitha as a widow before she had turned eighteen years of age.

Much to her surprise, her husband—who had never shown any sort of consideration for her—had ensured that she would be provided for should he die before her, leaving her with a small yet comfortable home in the country. The townhouse, she was permitted use of during the Season given that the newly appointed Lord Croome and his wife were rather aged, with a son already married and well settled. A yearly allowance meant that she was able to live a very contented life and, as yet, had nothing whatsoever to complain of.

"That is all you have to say?" Lady Pellingham asked, one eyebrow lifting in evident astonishment. "You state that this is, in fact, your third Season, but you have no intention of doing anything particular this summer?"

"I do not know what it is you expect of me," Tabitha replied honestly. "I am simply here to enjoy the Season and to reacquaint myself with the very dear friends that I have missed these last few months." Smiling brightly at Lady Pellingham, she waited in the hope that the astonished, if not slightly condemning, look would fade from the lady's face, only to see a dark frown begin to sweep itself across Lady Pellingham's forehead.

"Do you mean to tell me that you have no intention of finding yourself another suitable match?" Lady

Pellingham asked, her voice rising a little. "That this is your third Season here in London since you lost your dear husband, and that all you intend to do is simply *enjoy* yourself?" She threw up her hands and shook her head in evident horror. "That is not at all suitable for a young lady such as yourself!"

Tabitha blinked in surprise, not quite certain what she was to say in response. She had never once expected to hear such things from Lady Pellingham, for there had never been a particularly strong acquaintance between them. Rather, there had been an introduction and an occasional remark but nothing other than that.

"You shall have to think seriously about your future, Lady Croome," continued Lady Pellingham, her chin lifting haughtily. "I think it best that you seek a husband for yourself. It is not right for a young lady to be going about town in such a manner."

Tabitha did not know what to say, but it seemed she was to have no time to make any further remark, for Lady Pellingham turned on her heel to make her way to the door of the shop, leaving Tabitha standing, stunned, in her wake.

"Good gracious," Lady Ashbrook whispered, startling Tabitha from her astonishment. "I believe everyone in the vicinity heard Lady Pellingham's judgment upon you!" Moving around to face Tabitha a little more, she looked at her with wide eyes. "Whatever shall you do?"

Giving herself a slight shake and, realizing that the other ladies in the shop were now either whispering to each other about what they had seen or watching Tabitha carefully, she gave what she hoped was a careless shrug and then smiled as brightly as she could.

"I shall not do anything except what I intend to do," she replied firmly. "Whilst I appreciate Lady Pellingham's intentions, there is nothing that I need to concern myself with. Her concern is very kindly meant, I am sure, but I fully expect to continue with the Season just as I have planned."

Lady Ashbrook's eyes remained just as wide as before. "Do you think that is wise?" she asked, lowering her voice as the others in the shop began to converse normally again, given that they had now heard Tabitha speak as she had done. "Lady Pellingham can easily have one thrown from the favor of society, should she so wish it."

"I doubt that she would do such a thing to me simply because I refused to find a husband," Tabitha replied firmly. "Come now, Dinah, push such thoughts and concern from your mind and let us instead think of what we came here to do." She chuckled and took Lady Ashbrook's arm. "To find you a few new items so that you will simply *dazzle* your husband at whatever events you attend."

Lady Ashbrook laughed, and the tension that had hung over Tabitha's head shattered in an instant. She had no need to concern herself with Lady Pellingham's words, she told herself. There was nothing to worry her here, for she was convinced that Lady Pellingham would forget about her remarks in a few days time. There would be many others that she would have cause to consider, many other young ladies who would fall foul of her high standards of propriety! As she picked up a new pair of silk gloves, Tabitha let out a breath she had not known she had been holding. Yes, there was nothing to worry about this Season, she was quite sure of it. Everything would be as she had planned.

CHAPTER ONE

"And so you are to meet with your solicitors?"

Oliver harrumphed, glancing at his friend. "It does sound rather sinister, does it not?" he muttered as Lord Jennings chuckled. "You may laugh, but I am not entirely pleased with the situation."

Lord Jennings shrugged as they meandered through London's Hyde Park. "It is just that you have seen your solicitors many times over these last few years," he said as Oliver let out a groan of frustration. "Your father was, if it is not rude to say, one of the most eccentric gentlemen I ever had the opportunity to meet."

Oliver did not say anything in response but knew all too well what Lord Jennings was speaking of. His late father had been bizarre, particularly in his later years. Over the last four years, instead of being able to settle into his new role as Earl of Yarmouth, he had been continually hounded by his solicitors who, in going through his father's papers, had found new wills which needed to be studied and considered, to see whether or not they superseded the one Oliver had at present. In addition, he had also found some wills, signed in his father's well-known handwriting, and thus had been forced to surrender them to the solicitors also. Whether or not this particular will would improve on the one they had in place at present, Oliver could not say.

"Correct me if I am mistaken," Lord Jennings continued, his tone bright and breezy, whereas Oliver felt nothing other than heavy dismay. "But the will that you are under at present states that you must be engaged within six months, does it not?"

Oliver rolled his eyes, fully aware that his friend was doing nothing more than attempting to irritate him with his question. "Yes, I am to be engaged within six months if I am to gain a large proportion of my late father's wealth," he grated, hating how such a large sum had been held back from him without any true cause. "Else it shall go to some undeserving cousin of mine, if I remember correctly."

"An excellent incentive, perhaps," Lord Jennings replied, one brow lifting slightly. "So, you are in London this Season in the hope of finding a bride?"

"I have no other choice unless you are better able than my solicitors to find a way for me to be free of it!" Oliver retorted scathingly. "It is not a situation that I am particularly pleased about, in case you are unaware."

"I am well aware of it," Lord Jennings replied, an infuriating grin spreading across his face. "It is something that brings me a good deal of mirth, given just how unwilling you are to even *consider* the debutantes this Season—or in any other Season, in fact."

Oliver did not immediately respond to this, thinking silently to himself that he had been unwilling to look at the debutantes given that he found them all to be much too flighty, much too wide-eyed and astonished with all that went on in London. No, if he was to take a wife, he would rather a lady who was perhaps on her second or even third Season and who was fully intending now to find a match. Someone willing to settle down into married life rather than being eager to return to London for all the enjoyments that it might provide.

"You are looking serious," Lord Jennings said, breaking into Oliver's thoughts. His face flushed as Oliver glanced at him, clearly now a little embarrassed. "I did not mean to frustrate you."

"Yes, you did," Oliver replied firmly. "You very much enjoy taking advantage of my situation in your own way, although I presume your attempts to make light of it are meant to encourage me." Shaking his head, he shot Lord Jennings a hard glance. "But it does nothing other than irritate me, Jennings. I find that I am greatly irritated at my circumstances, and I cannot understand why my father would stipulate such a thing in his will. It is more than a little trying, particularly when I would like to take my time about such an important thing as matrimony." Another glance was sent in his friend's direction, clearly warning him that he was *not* to mention the fact that Oliver could very well have done something about engaging himself to a young lady *last* Season, for it was something Oliver himself was very well aware of. He had hoped desperately that another will would be discovered that would free him from such a trial, but, as yet, it had not done so.

"Then I shall stop being so mirthful about it all," Lord Jennings decided. "I apologize, Yarmouth."

Oliver accepted it readily enough, fully aware that Lord Jennings was a gentleman who was always inclined towards finding the humorous side of things, even in the worst of situations. It was unfortunate, however, that Oliver himself did not find anything particularly funny about his present circumstances, else he might have appreciated a little levity.

"The park is certainly quiet this afternoon," Lord Jennings commented, now clearly attempting to remove the conversation from Oliver's difficulties into something much more banal. "I would have thought that the *beau monde* would have been eagerly waiting to descend upon it."

Oliver chuckled, and the remaining tension between himself and Lord Jennings shattered in an instant. "You forget that it is not yet the fashionable hour," he reminded his friend. "They will all be waiting to appear at the best opportunity to be seen as well as to make certain they can pay attention to everyone else present." He shrugged. "If we return to the carriage, we can take a turn about London and then return at the same time, so that we might take note as to who else is present for the Season this year."

"But surely that is not something you are inclined towards?" Lord Jennings retorted, throwing a curious glance towards Oliver. "You have never once wished to do such a thing before."

"And nor shall I do this Season either, no matter how much I might wish to find a suitable match," Oliver replied resolutely. "The fashionable hour is nothing but a crush of people all seeking to be noticed by others, and I shall not be a part of it." A small shudder ran through his frame, but he set his shoulders and lifted his chin. "Which means, I suppose, that I shall have to find a young lady entirely unwilling to seek out such things also."

Lord Jennings said nothing but, from the expression on his face, Oliver guessed that his friend did not think that such a thing was likely. He could not blame him. The many ladies of the *beau monde* were eager to be noticed by others in the *ton*—particularly if they held a lower title and sought to marry off their daughters to a gentleman of a greater one—and therefore, would not turn away from the fashionable hour at Hyde Park! It would be almost impossible to find such a creature, Oliver admitted to himself, but he was determined that he should try. If he were to be engaged with the expectation of marriage, then he was quite certain that the lady he chose for himself had to be tolerable, at the very least! And that meant that she needed particular qualities in order for him to find her so.

"Can it be?"

A voice ahead of him stopped him in his tracks, the sun shining in his eyes and making it difficult for him to make out the face of the lady approaching him.

"It is!" the voice said again, sounding truly delighted to see him—and instantly, Oliver knew who it was.

"Lady Croome!" he exclaimed, finally able to make

out her features as she drew closer. "How very good to see you!" He took her outstretched hand and bowed low over it, wishing that he could embrace her in a much too familiar fashion. "You are returned to London, then?"

Lady Croome laughed, her brown eyes sparkling in the afternoon sunshine as her dark curls blew lightly in the wind, framing her face as they did so. "It appears I have," she answered as he begrudgingly let go of her hand. Quickly, she reminded him of his previous acquaintance with her friend, Lady Ashbrook, greeting Lord Jennings before continuing their conversation. "And you are back in London also?" Her eyes studied his face, although her lips remained in a small smile.

"Yes, yes, I am here for the Season," he confirmed, grinning at her as she beamed at him. "I very much hope to be in your acquaintance again, as we have been these last two Seasons."

Sighing, Lady Croome put a hand on her heart in a most dramatic fashion as Lady Ashbrook giggled, her cheeks going a little pink as Oliver glanced at her.

"Well, Lord Yarmouth, I am not entirely certain that I shall be able to do so," she said in a dramatic tone. "Lady Pellingham has only just informed me that I should seek out a husband this Season, stating that it is not quite the thing for a lady to remain widowed without any hope of further prospects," she told him with yet another sigh. "And given that it is Lady Pellingham who has spoken this decree, I feel quite obliged to do as she states."

Oliver chuckled, shaking his head at her. "Is that so?" he replied disbelievingly. "Do you fear you will be thrown from society otherwise?"

"Good gracious, I do hope not!" Lady Croome replied, her eyes widening now. "You do know, of course, that I have no intention of doing what Lady Pellingham asks, but I certainly hope that she will not think poorly of me for refusing to do as she thinks best."

Considering this, Oliver paused for a few moments to reflect before lifting one shoulder in a half shrug. "Lady Pellingham will, I am sure, be very distracted by all the other young ladies who have never yet been wed," he said, as Lord Jennings and Lady Ashbrook began to speak quietly to each other, leaving him to speak freely to Lady Croome. "I do not think that you have anything particular to worry about."

This seemed to bring a great relief to Lady Croome, for she let out a long breath and gave him what appeared to be a genuine smile of relief.

"It was shocking, I will admit," she said, taking a small step closer to him and speaking in a lower tone of voice so that she would not be overheard. "I was shopping with Lady Ashbrook, only to be approached by Lady Pellingham and told, directly, that this was what I should do this Season. She appeared quite confounded when I stated I had no intention of finding another husband!"

"I do not know why she believes she has such power," Oliver replied in what he hoped was a comforting manner. "Ignore what she stated and go about the Season as you have planned. It shall all come aright soon enough, I am sure."

Lady Croome studied him for a moment or two before she smiled and nodded, looking away from him so that she might look out over the park. It gave Oliver time to study her familiar features, grateful beyond measure to see his dear friend again.

She had not changed even a little, he realized, taking in her oval face, her slender neck, and delicate frame. Her eyes were just as warm as they had always been, her smile ever ready and her countenance as delightful as ever. Seeing her again brought a warmth to Oliver's soul and, for a few minutes at least, his troubles seemed to be fading away.

"Tell me, Lord Yarmouth," Lady Croome said, looking back at him with what appeared to be a concerned expression. "Have you found any further wills?"

Shaking his head, Oliver glanced at Lord Jennings but saw, much to his relief, that his friend was busy conversing with Lady Ashbrook still.

"None," he replied, aware of the hint of bitterness in his words that left a sharp taste in his mouth. "I am to be engaged by the sixth month; else I shall not receive the rest of my father's fortune."

Lady Croome's expression filled with sympathy, and she put one hand out to rest on his arm for a moment. "I am sorry," she said kindly. "If there were anything I could do, then I can assure you that I would do so."

"I know that your good heart is eager to assist me," he told her, grateful for her consideration. "But it seems as though I have no choice." Sighing, he looked out across Hyde Park, unwilling to speak the words he knew were now before him, unwilling to release him from their grip. "It seems that, this Season, I must find myself a bride."

"Then I shall do all I can to advise you," Lady

Croome replied with a firmness in her voice that made him smile. "Although I cannot be sure that any of my judgments will be useful!"

He laughed, seeing the twinkle in her eyes and knowing that she was doing all she could to encourage him. "I will be grateful for them all the same," he answered, as Lady Ashbrook and Lord Jennings finished their conversation and returned their attention to them both. "Tell me, Lady Croome, will you be attending Lord Barchester's ball tomorrow evening?"

"I intend to, yes," Lady Croome replied, the smile on her lips and the gleam in her eyes telling him that she remembered the many enjoyable evenings they had spent together last Season. "Shall you seek me out, mayhap?"

"I shall do so the moment I enter," he told her as she laughed softly. "Then, you can do as you have done before and save me from the many young ladies who come to seek me out—or whose mothers come to do so!"

"And you shall protect me from Lady Pellingham!" came the swift reply. "It is not only you who shall need to hide oneself away for a time this year, Lord Yarmouth! It seems I may have to do so also!"

"Then we shall be of assistance to each other," he told her as she inclined her head in evident thanks. "Until tomorrow evening, then. Good afternoon, Lady Croome. Lady Ashbrook." He inclined his head, and the two ladies dropped into a quick curtsy.

"Good afternoon, Lord Yarmouth, Lord Jennings," Lady Croome replied, her smile still fixed to her lips as she made her way past them both and continued on their walk through the park.

"There is your answer!"

Oliver blinked rapidly, looking at his friend in startled confusion. "Whatever do you mean?"

Lord Jennings threw up his hands in exasperation. "Wed Lady Croome!" he explained, just as Oliver began to laugh. "Why should you think that such an idea is foolishness? She is a widow, which means she is not a debutante, nor someone who seeks to put on fine airs in order to catch a husband. She is very much inclined towards your company, as you are to hers, and, besides which, she has a great deal of beauty, which I am *certain* you cannot deny!"

"I do not deny it," Oliver replied with a grin. "But Lady Croome is nothing more than a friend. Surely you have seen how our acquaintance has developed over the last two Seasons?" He smiled to himself, remembering the first time he had been introduced to Lady Croome. She had none of the confidence that practically exuded from her today but had been quiet and, in fact, a little shy. Her husband had died, and, after her year of mourning, she had been attempting to find her role in society as a widow. Something about her vulnerable state had spoken to his heart, and Oliver had found himself wanting to improve their acquaintance. That acquaintance had grown into a friendship that he very much enjoyed, and there had never once been any sort of suggestion between them that they might consider something more. To do so now, he reasoned, would bring an end to the wonderful friendship that they both currently enjoyed, and that was a thought he could not bear to even consider.

"I have seen your acquaintance and your friendship, yes," Lord Jennings replied, "but that does not mean that you should not consider her in a different light!" He stopped dead, and Oliver was forced to stop walking also, turning to Lord Jennings with a heavy sigh issuing from his lips.

"You are only required to be engaged, is that not so?" Lord Jennings asked pointedly, his eyes flaring with excitement that Oliver could not understand.

"Indeed, that is the agreement," Oliver replied, spreading his hands. "As you well know."

"Then why not engage yourself to Lady Croome?" Lord Jennings asked. "It need not last. It need only satisfy the terms made in the will, which means that once you receive the remainder of the wealth, then there will be no further need to continue with the engagement."

Oliver opened his mouth to refute the idea, only to close it again. His brow began to furrow as he considered all that Lord Jennings had suggested, realizing, with shock, that it was an almost perfect solution.

One glance towards his friend told him that Lord Jennings was all too aware that his idea held a great deal of merit and, indeed, he himself had to admit that there was no flaw in the plan. Lady Croome would be open to helping him, he was sure, for she had said so herself only a few minutes ago. Whether or not he could convince her to engage herself to him—albeit quietly—he was not certain, although surely, if she knew that it would soon come to an end, she would not have any particular reason for disagreement.

"I should only have to engage myself to her for a few

short weeks," he said aloud as Lord Jennings nodded eagerly. "I know the date well enough that I must find myself engaged and could, therefore, propose even a day or so before then."

"Meaning that you would have only a week's engagement before you could bring things to a close," Lord Jennings agreed. "And thus decided, the Season is laid out before you just as it has been before—with merriment, enjoyment, and excitement rather than anxiety, worry, and a requirement to seek out a bride." His brow lifted, and his eyes twinkled and, despite Oliver's determination not to tell Lord Jennings the truth about just how good his particular suggestion was, Oliver found himself grinning broadly, reaching out to slap his friend on the shoulder.

"Capital!" he exclaimed as Lord Jennings chuckled. "A capital idea, Jennings!" A long breath of relief escaped him. "I believe you have saved me entirely."

"I do hope so," Lord Jennings replied, his mouth quirking. "For mayhap, now you will stop with your moping and your melancholy and instead return to the Season with the expectation of enjoyment rather than dread!"

"I can think of nothing better," Oliver replied steadfastly. "And now I need only approach Lady Croome!" His stomach twisted at the thought, but he took a deep breath, steadying himself as he did so. "I am *certain* that she will agree."

Lord Jennings laughed and began to walk forward again. "If anyone is willing to do so for your sake, it will be Lady Croome," he told Oliver, reminding him of Lady

Croome's loyalty towards him in her friendship. "Let us hope, for your sake, that her loyalty will prove itself to you in this."

"Indeed," Oliver breathed, feeling a sense of relief wrap itself around his shoulders like a warm blanket. "Let us hope it will be as you say."

CHAPTER TWO

"Lord Yarmouth has not yet arrived?"

Tabitha looked across the ballroom once more, but her attempts to secure Lord Yarmouth failed miserably.

"He has not," she answered with a grimace. "And I am quite sure that Lady Pellingham remains close to me in order to make quite certain that I am engaging myself with suitable gentlemen."

Lady Ashbrook glanced up at her husband, who merely rolled his eyes but said nothing more. Tabitha smiled to herself but kept her gaze roving around the room, wanting desperately to find Lord Yarmouth's familiar features. Lord and Lady Ashbrook were the very best of people, she considered, and very well suited in their match together. Lord Ashbrook was a gentleman who spoke very little, but what he did say was always very profound. He clearly adored his wife, for his eyes would linger on her face whenever she looked away from his, his mouth lifting into a half-smile, and his gaze warm.

In return, Lady Ashbrook cared for her husband, her gaiety bringing him out of that staid appearance that so often shrouded him from society.

Would that her own marriage had been so! Tabitha had never been happy in her match, which, having been made for her by her father, had never once allowed her to have any say in the matter. Her husband, Lord Croome, had cared only for himself and his own pleasures and, whilst he had never been cruel towards her, had never shown any delight in her company or had been eager to seek her out.

"You are very dear friends, I think."

Looking back towards Lord Ashbrook, Tabitha nodded, a smile in her voice. "Lord Yarmouth and I have known each other for what is now three Seasons," she told him by way of explanation. "My first Season, he was very kind to me, and I discovered a strength and determination through his encouragement."

"And there is no sort of attachment between you?" Lord Ashbrook asked in an interested voice, which bore no condemnation. "You have nothing more there?"

Shaking her head, Tabitha kept her smile hidden. "No, indeed not," she replied evenly. "I am aware that it is not the done thing to have such a friendship between a lady of the *ton* and a gentleman, but I have discovered that, with my current status, I can do such a thing without too much fear of reprimand or reproach to others." Reminded of Lady Pellingham, she glanced over her shoulder only to see that the lady was still standing in the very same spot, although her eyes were fixed to someone who was, at present, conversing with another.

"I see," Lord Ashbrook replied with a small lift of his shoulders. "You are quite right to state that it is not the expected thing, Lady Croome, but that does not mean that it cannot take place."

"I am very glad you think so," Tabitha replied with a genuine smile of thanks. "I should not like to bring any sort of shame to either myself or to Lord Yarmouth, but there is nothing of importance between us, save for an excellent friendship I am very grateful for."

Lady Ashbrook let out a small sigh and shook her head. "I do not think such a friendship will last, however," she warned as Tabitha frowned, not understanding what her friend meant. "Once he is wed, there can be none of what you have at present."

Tabitha's eyes flared, and her cheeks began to warm with embarrassment, fully aware of what her friend meant. "Of course, I quite understand that!" she exclaimed, eager not to give the impression that she intended to continue with her close friendship with Lord Yarmouth once he was engaged or wed. She had already thought of such a thing and had decided that she would, of course, step away from Lord Yarmouth the moment he began courting a young lady in earnest. It would not do for her to continue her friendship with him in such a way, for no doubt, society would think worse of them both for it. Crude suggestions would be made, whispers and rumors would chase them both, and she did not want that for him or for the lady he would one day marry.

"That is wise of you to have thought of such a situation before, then," Lady Ashbrook replied with evident relief in her voice. "Now, Lord Ashbrook, are we to remain standing here all night, or do you wish to waltz with me?"

Tabitha watched as Lord Ashbrook started gently, clearly unaware of the fact that the music was a waltz. His face flushed just a little, and he bowed towards his wife, offering her his hand, which she took at once, an eager smile on her face and a brightness in her eyes that made Tabitha's heart squeeze with happiness for her friend. She was glad indeed that there was such contentment in Lady Ashbrook's marriage and, watching them leave to dance together, felt a sudden sting of envy.

"You should not stand there in such a forlorn manner."

Tabitha laughed, turning her head to see Lord Yarmouth standing behind her, just lifting his head from a bow, his hand outstretched.

"We have not waltzed in a long time, Lord Yarmouth," she replied teasingly. "What if you stand on my toes and bring about such pain that I will be forced to limp from the floor?"

He grinned at her, his brown eyes seeming to light with flecks of gold for a moment or two. "That is a risk you shall have to take, Lady Croome," he told her, as she took his hand. "Although I think you shall find that I am just as good at waltzing as I have ever been."

Tabitha laughed and allowed him to lead her onto the floor. It was just as well, given that she had seen, out of the corner of her eye, Lady Pellingham beginning to advance towards her, no doubt ready to ensure that Tabitha's dance card was sufficiently filled.

"You have rescued me once again, it seems," Tabitha

chuckled as the music began. "I see Lady Pellingham was about to speak to me again."

"I do not think that she will consider me to be suitable company for you, however," Lord Yarmouth replied with a grin, one hand settling on her waist. "For you know very well that I am a gentleman who has been in London for some years and still not yet thought to court a single young lady!"

Dimpling, Tabitha caught her breath as he spun her around the floor. Lord Yarmouth had always been an excellent dancer, and this evening, it seemed, was no different. The brightness of his eyes and the quirk of his lips told her that he was pleased with their success on the dance floor, garnering some glances from the crowd who noticed them on the floor.

"You are quite right," she told him, managing to get her breath back enough to speak. "You certainly would *not* be suitable company, according to Lady Pellingham." Her own lips curved as Lord Yarmouth tutted loudly, his hand still clasping hers tightly. "Although, if you would be so good as to deposit me somewhere other than near to the lady once the dance is ended, I should be very grateful."

"I will remain by your side, if you wish it," Lord Yarmouth replied, his steps still sure and swift as he held her tightly. "Just as we have done many times before."

Tabitha's eyes twinkled. "But this Season is very different, is it not?" she pointed out, one eyebrow arching. "You are to find a young lady to propose to so that you might fulfill your father's wishes."

She watched him closely, surprised when he did not

immediately agree but rather looked away from her. The music began to slow, and Lord Yarmouth did also, making certain to stay in time with the music until the final few notes drifted away. Releasing her, Lord Yarmouth applauded the orchestra politely, as did she, before dropping into a bow.

"Thank you very much, Lord Yarmouth," Tabitha murmured as she rose from her curtsy and immediately took his arm. "I do hope I did not upset you by mentioning your particular situation." Her heart squeezed painfully as he looked down sharply at her, worrying that she had done just that. "It is a matter of seriousness, of which I am fully aware of. Forgive me for speaking of it lightly."

Lord Yarmouth smiled at her softly, reaching across to pat her hand as he led her through the other guests to a quieter part of the room. "It is not your teasing that has made me so quiet," he told her, allowing her to let out a sigh of relief. "Rather, it is the very matter itself that brings about a disquiet within my heart."

"Would that I could do something to be of aid," Tabitha replied honestly. "I know that you do not desire to marry as yet."

He turned to her, and the look in his eyes startled her, for it was not an expression she had seen often on his face. His brow was furrowed, his dark brown hair brushing across it as he gazed at her steadily. His mouth was pulled tight, and there was almost a sense of foreboding coming from him. Tabitha tried to find something to say, something to ask him as to why he appeared so, but instead found that her throat was closing. Therefore, being forced to wait, she felt a tension seizing her, her heart beginning to thunder furiously as, with each second that passed, she felt herself grow all the more anxious as to what he was to say.

"It is no use." Lord Yarmouth dropped his head into one hand, his fingers pushing through his hair as, with an expression of irritation, he let out a loud groan and looked back at her. "It does not matter, Tabitha. Please, let us speak of something else."

It was not often that Lord Yarmouth used her given name, although, of course, she had given him permission to do so. This told her that there was something of great importance on Lord Yarmouth's mind and, whilst she fully expected it to be merely the situation that faced him in terms of his engagement, there was something more in his expression. Something that, she feared, he would not express to her unless she pressed him to do so.

"You are being mysterious, and I do not much like it," she told him firmly, putting one hand on his arm for a moment so that he would look into her eyes. "What is it that troubles you?"

Lord Yarmouth held her gaze for a moment and then threw up his hands. "Lord Jennings gave me an idea as to how I might find a way through this particular situation without being forced into matrimony with a lady I care nothing for," he said slowly as Tabitha felt her curiosity stir. "At first, I thought it a capital idea, but now that I am standing before you, ready to explain it, I find that I cannot do so."

A little confused, Tabitha frowned up at him. "And why is that?"

"Because it might very well ruin all that we enjoy at present," he explained, although such an explanation did not make much sense to her. "What if our friendship is ruined by such an idea?"

Growing a little frustrated and wishing desperately that her heart would slow its rapid pace, Tabitha let her frown linger. "You need to tell me precisely what Lord Jennings has suggested," she said resolutely, her chin lifting just a little. "You know very well that I am determined enough that I shall hear it from you whether you wish to tell me of it or not!"

This statement brought a wry smile to Lord Yarmouth's lips, and he nodded, although he did not immediately say anything to her. Instead, his eyes dropped to her shoulder and then to someone or something just behind her as though too embarrassed or uncertain to look her directly in the eye.

"That is true enough, I suppose," he told her, a heaviness about his expression. "You must assure me, however, that you will believe that I have no intention of following through with Lord Jennings' idea, unless, of course, you think that it would be a wise suggestion."

Tabitha nodded, looking at her friend steadily. "I quite understand," she said, still having very little idea as to what this particular suggestion might be and why it sent Lord Yarmouth into such a strange manner. "What is it that Lord Jennings believes I can do to assist you?"

Lord Yarmouth pressed his lips together and then shrugged. "He thinks that you and I might become engaged," he said, surprising her completely. "Not that there is any intention of us to wed, of course, but that we might remain engaged in order to fulfill the requirement of my father's will. Thereafter, we shall cry off, and it will all be done in a calm fashion, without any particular fuss."

Tabitha let out her breath slowly, seeing the embarrassment in Lord Yarmouth's face and feeling a sense of awkwardness filling her.

"You do not know what to say," Lord Yarmouth muttered, pushing yet another hand through his hair. "That is to be expected. It is a foolish suggestion and, whilst I accepted it eagerly from Lord Jennings, it is not one that I would ever expect you to—"

"I shall think on it."

Lord Yarmouth stopped dead, looking at her with wide, astonished eyes.

"It *is* a wise suggestion," Tabitha found herself saying, surprising even herself with her reply. "For it would not mean anything of significance, I suppose."

"No, no," Lord Yarmouth said quickly, one hand slicing the air between them. "It would be only a matter of requirement rather than it having any significance of its own."

"And we would keep it all very quiet indeed," Tabitha continued, seeing Lord Yarmouth nod fervently. "So there would be no damage to either reputation thereafter. Not substantial damage, at least."

Lord Yarmouth did not reply, looking at her with such intensity that Tabitha did not know how to respond to him. Was he seeking to be certain that she knew precisely what she was speaking of? Did he perhaps think that she might immediately change her mind once she had allowed herself to think on it a little more?

"I know that we are very dear friends, and, whilst our friendship is unusual within society, I hope you know that I would be very glad indeed to do whatever is required in order to help you," she told him as Lord Yarmouth began to nod slowly. "Allow me to think on it a little longer, but I am certain that I shall be quite accepting of the situation."

Giving her a small shake of his head, Lord Yarmouth's lips tipped into a rueful smile. "You are quite an extraordinary lady, Tabitha," he told her, with all the fondness of a dear friend. "I could not even bring myself to ask you such a thing, fearful that it would be too much of a burden, but you have accepted it without hesitation."

She smiled back at him, feeling her heart now settled into a calm rhythm, contented now that she knew all that had been troubling him. Part of her wondered why she had not thought of such a thing herself but was, instead, grateful to Lord Jennings for his clarity of mind. There was almost a relief in her agreeing to his suggestion, for she knew very well that Lord Yarmouth did not want to be forced into matrimony when he did not feel it yet a requirement to do so. Being a gentleman with his own mind and singular determination, she had heard many times over how the various wills that kept revealing themselves were a cumbersome burden indeed and wanted, truly, to do whatever she could to lighten that burden somewhat.

"The engagement would not have to take place until the end of the Season, if not a little after that," he told her as she shrugged. "It would be of short duration and only to fulfill the requirement of my father's will."

"I am quite contented with that," she replied, noting how a particular young lady and her mother were beginning to make their way carefully towards Lord Yarmouth, clearly unwilling to appear overeager but still determined to greet him. "Perhaps, however, we should speak on such matters at a later date." Her eyes twinkled as she saw him frown. "There appear to be others who are eager for your company, Lord Yarmouth."

A giggle left her mouth as Lord Yarmouth twisted his head this way and that, only to alight on the young lady in question. An expression of horror ran through his features, and he turned back to face her, wide-eyed and with a paleness to his cheeks that had not been there before.

"You must rescue me!" he exclaimed as Tabitha arched one eyebrow questioningly. "Lady Millerton is quite determined to marry me to her *dreadful* daughter and has hounded me since the very moment she returned to London!"

"Well, I would suggest we might dance," Tabitha replied with a shrug, "but that would be one after the other and certainly would be remarked upon." She could not help but laugh again as the two ladies drew nearer, leaving Lord Yarmouth almost frantic with the desperate desire to escape without any particular ability to do so. "Mayhap, we could go in search of Lady Ashbrook?"

He grasped her arm almost at once. "An excellent idea," he whispered before stating loudly, "but of course,

Lady Croome, I should be glad to return you to Lady Ashbrook. Let us walk this way."

Tabitha hid a smile as she walked directly past Lady Millerton and her unfortunate daughter, who both watched Lord Yarmouth with equal expressions of frustration mixed with an obvious desire to draw near to him —although, for entirely different reasons, of course.

"You have saved me once again, Lady Croome," Lord Yarmouth breathed, clearly relieved to have been saved from them both. "It seems as though this Season is to go very much the same way as last year's!"

"Indeed it does," Tabitha replied, her arm now looped comfortably through his. "And that, Lord Yarmouth, I consider to be an excellent thing indeed."

CHAPTER THREE

Lord Jennings grinned broadly and stretched his arms high above his head before relaxing back into his chair again. "Then it seems that you owe me a great deal of appreciation," he said with a lift of his eyebrows. "For if I had not made the suggestion, then I do not think that you would have ever come to such a conclusion yourself!"

Try as he might, Oliver could not think of a rebuttal to this, sighing heavily and rolling his eyes as Lord Jennings waited expectantly.

"Very well," he admitted as Lord Jennings' grin spread all the wider. "You have done very well, Jennings. I will be truthful: I did not expect Lady Croome to agree, but she has done so!" He smiled to himself, picking up the note that he had received earlier that morning and gesturing with it towards Lord Jennings. "She states that she will do precisely what I have asked without hesitation, so long as the date of our engagement does not take place within the Season itself."

"Very wise," Lord Jennings agreed, picking up his glass of whisky from the nearby table and swirling the liquid around. "There should be very little talk of it so that none in the *ton* are aware and can hold it against you when the time comes to cry off."

Oliver chuckled, sitting back in his seat and feeling as though the world had finally set itself to rights. He had been given a reprieve. There was no need to jump into a hasty engagement and marriage! He had his freedom still and could choose a wife at a time that suited him best. All was contentment once again, and he could not help but feel a great deal of relief capturing his heart, soul, and mind as one.

"Then might I ask," Lord Jennings said slowly, no longer wearing that broad grin that usually irritated Oliver so much, "whether or not you hold any concern regarding the visit of your solicitors in..." He glanced at the clock. "Ah, in only a few minutes' time?"

"I do not think they shall have anything further to say," Oliver replied with a shrug. "Or, if they do, I doubt very much that there shall be any significant changes to the will at present. After all, the last three wills have all stated the very same: that I must be engaged by this particular time if I am to gain the rest of my father's fortune." He rolled his eyes to himself, half wishing that he could berate his father for his eccentricity in doing such a thing. There had been a fondness between father and son but nothing of any great depth, and, in the latter years of his father's life, Oliver had found himself growing tired of his strange notions. For the last few years, there had been nothing but confusion and doubt over what was now expected of him, with the solicitors apologizing profusely each and every time a new will was discovered. It was not their doing, of course, and whilst Oliver did not hold it against them, it was all becoming wearying.

"So you are quite certain that this will, if it is a new one they have discovered, will state the same as the last three have done?" Lord Jennings asked, just as a scratch came at the door."

"I am sure there will be a few changes, but nothing of significance," Oliver replied honestly. "My father wanted me to be engaged and settled, it seems, and I can hardly imagine that he would go back on such a thing in later documents." Seeing Lord Jennings rising to leave, he gestured for him to remain sitting. "There is no need for you to depart," he said before calling the butler in. "I am sure this visit will not take long."

Lord Jennings sank back into his chair gratefully, whilst the butler walked in and announced one Mr. Irving, whom Oliver knew rather well. The man was short and wiry, with thinning gray hair, a somewhat pointed nose, and sharp green eyes that always unsettled Oliver somewhat. He knew Mr. Irving to be direct and blunt, leaving the others in his firm to apologize continually to Oliver over what had occurred. Oliver appreciated his manner even if he was not ever truly glad to see him.

"Mr. Irving," he said once the formal greetings had been passed. "Please sit down." He gestured to a chair, and Mr. Irving took it at once, clearing his throat just a little as he did so.

"I have unfortunate news, Lord Yarmouth," Mr.

Irving began in a practical manner. "As you know, the solicitor who dealt with your father's will was, regrettably, a little too eager to do all that the earl asked without question or guidance. He was quite willing to go along with this scheme, and, due to his death a short time after your own honorable father, we are unable to find out just how many wills were written." He cleared his throat again, and Oliver found himself holding his breath, wondering just what would be revealed to him now. "However," Mr. Irving said in a grand manner, "we have discovered, Lord Yarmouth, another will amongst the final lot of your father's many, many papers."

"Indeed," Oliver said, not understanding the almost proud expression on the man's face. "And is this one dated later than the one we have at present?"

Mr. Irving's lips twitched. "It is signed and dated as the day before the earl passed away," he said, pulling it out and handing it to Oliver with a slight bow of his head. "As you know, your father's papers were substantial and without order, which is why it has taken us some time to discover it. However, I am quite certain that there can be no other wills present, Lord Yarmouth. This, I believe, is the final will that the late Earl of Yarmouth wrote, and it is with this that I now present you."

Gesturing to it, Mr. Irving kept his head bowed until Oliver leaned forward and picked it up, feeling a sense of triumph beginning to rise in his chest. The nightmare, it seemed, was at an end. Drawing in a deep breath and seeing Lord Jennings lift his glass in a silent toast, Oliver grinned at his friend and then slowly unrolled the paper.

It began just as the others had done. There were

specifics about various servants, grants, bequests, and the like that Oliver was to fulfill. There was also mention of a great aunt and her daughter, which Oliver had not read before. Evidently, in his last few hours on this earth, the late Earl had recalled some family members that he had previously forgotten.

His eyes strayed to the last paragraph, fully expecting it to be the very same as before.

His heart seemed to stop in his chest, his hands cold as he grasped the paper tightly. Over and over, he read the words, reading them furiously as he slowly began to realize what his father had done.

There had been a change—a significant one at that. No longer was he to merely become *engaged* in six months: he was to be wed. Married. Settled. Else he would not receive the final portion of his father's fortune.

"I know it is something of a change," he heard Mr. Irving say, the quietness of his voice sounding as though he spoke from very far away. "But if you are already engaged, then that does not pose a significant problem."

Oliver closed his eyes and set the paper down on the table, wishing he could rip the whole thing apart.

"I am not engaged as yet," he whispered, opening his eyes to see Lord Jennings rising to his feet, a look of alarm on his face.

Mr. Irving cleared his throat for what was now the third time and rose slowly from his chair, spreading his hands in a manner that spoke of his lack of ability to change anything that was written therein. "That is the will we must now abide by, Lord Yarmouth," he said solemnly. "I am sorry, but there is nothing further I can do."

Oliver got to his feet and, with what felt like a great effort, reached out to shake Mr. Irving's hand. It was not the good solicitor's fault that he was in this particular situation, nor was it his doing that a final will had been found that altered the previous. And yet Oliver wanted desperately to find someone to blame, someone he might go to in order to allow his rage to be fully expressed in words.

"Thank you, Mr. Irving," he said with as much firmness as he could muster. "I appreciate you coming to inform me of this."

Mr. Irving nodded but did not turn to take his leave as Oliver had expected. Instead, he held Oliver's gaze, looking at him steadily, his head slightly tilted.

"Might I ask, Lord Yarmouth, whether or not you intend to fulfill the requirements of this particular will?" he asked, his question direct. "I shall make the necessary arrangements, of course, if you plan on marrying soon."

"I have every intention of fulfilling my late father's stringent requests," Oliver bit out, doing his utmost to keep his temper under control. "Be assured that I shall be a married gentleman before the six months are over."

A glimmer of a smile appeared around Mr. Irving's mouth, and his gaze softened just a fraction. "Then I shall make sure that on your wedding day, Lord Yarmouth, you will receive the outstanding amount of your father's wealth," he said with a sharp bow. "Good afternoon."

"Good afternoon," Oliver muttered, placing both hands on his desk and leaning forward, dropping his head low as he did so. The door closed with a firm click and, for some minutes, the only sound was the gentle ticking of the clock. Unfortunately, it only reminded Oliver of just how little time he now had to settle upon a wife, making his anger burn all the hotter as he stared down at the will with a furious eye.

"I—I am sorry," Lord Jennings said quietly, rising from his chair and walking across the room so that he might pour Oliver a whisky, which was then set down on the table in front of him. "Here."

Closing his eyes and dragging in another breath in the hope of calming his temper, Oliver opened them again and then picked up the glass of whisky.

"I thank you," he muttered, taking a long sip and letting it flood his core. It did nothing to dissipate his anger but quite how he was meant to remove it from himself, Oliver did not know.

"Then it seems our plans have been in vain," Lord Jennings said gloomily. "No doubt, you shall have to tell Lady Croome that all has been quite ruined."

"Indeed I shall," Oliver replied, throwing back the rest of his whisky and slamming down the glass, hard, making Lord Jennings jump with surprise. "Why my father thought to do such a thing, I shall *never* understand." Seeing how Lord Jennings looked at him with evident surprise at this remark, a flush of shame crept over Oliver's anger and began to soothe it somewhat. With a snort, he shook his head ruefully, his shoulders slumping. "Very well, you know precisely what sort of son I was and why, mayhap, my father then chose to place this caveat in his will."

Nodding, Lord Jennings went to fetch Oliver another whisky, leaving Oliver to throw himself back into his chair, slumping back as he did so. "Your father did ask you to find a bride before his death so that he could be assured of the continuation of your family line," he said, as Oliver grunted. "But you did not agree."

"I had no need to agree!" Oliver retorted as though he were verbally fencing with Lord Jennings. "I have the right to make my own choice of bride at the time that I consider to be the most appropriate."

"I am well aware of that," Lord Jennings replied, setting down the glass. "But your father did not agree with you from what I recall." He gave Oliver a wry smile. "Hence, the will."

Oliver nodded gloomily, looking at his whisky glass but not picking it up. "I am the only son, so I must produce the heir," he said darkly. "It is such a responsibility and one that, while I take seriously, will not force me into a situation I do not want at present."

Lord Jennings said nothing for a few moments, and Oliver knew all too well that his friend could not respond with criticism given that he was also titled and unmarried —without any apparent eagerness to do so.

"I think that, before anything else is done, you must speak to Lady Croome," Lord Jennings said quietly as Oliver frowned hard. "She will need to know of this change in circumstance."

"And will, most likely, be very relieved indeed," Oliver replied, reaching to pick up his whisky. "Although I know she will not be glad for me." An image of Lady Croome's gentle face floated before his eyes, and Oliver let out a small sigh. She would be kind, as she always was, and would speak words of comfort and encouragement, seeking to do whatever she could to assist him. It was only now that Oliver knew there was nothing at all that the lady herself could do, for it was quite impossible for anyone to be of assistance to him. The only path he had left before him was the one he had been trying to avoid for these last few months. There was no other choice but to choose a young lady from amongst the *beau monde*, court her, propose to her, and marry her. Else he would not have the remainder of his father's fortune.

"You do not think that she would...?" Lord Jennings did not finish his question but rather looked back at Oliver with a slight curiosity in his expression.

"Do I think that she would marry me?" he asked, ridicule already in his words. "Of course not! And I should not want her to do so either, for she is very contented indeed, and I would not take that from her." The very thought of Lady Croome being willing to marry him was laughable, and Oliver shook his head with mirth whilst Lord Jennings shrugged and muttered something about wanting to make quite certain that it was as he thought.

"Perhaps she will be able to assist you in finding a suitable match, then," Lord Jennings suggested once Oliver had stopped his chuckling. "After all, she is a lady of the *ton* and will know most of the debutantes this year."

"I do not want a debutante," Oliver began, but Lord Jennings silenced him with a lift of his hand.

"You must now set aside all that you believe that you

want or that you do not want," he said as though he were speaking to a very small child who was behaving in a most petulant fashion. "There are other matters of great importance to which you must set your mind. You may discover that, in your quest to find a lady who is quite satisfactory, you will settle upon a debutante rather than a young lady who has been in London before!" His eyes twinkled for a moment before the seriousness returned. "Tell me, Lord Yarmouth, what particular characteristics do you seek in a bride?"

It was not a question that Oliver had ever truly considered before. He had been so determined *not* to do so, desperately hoping that he could find a way through his father's demand for an engagement, and thus he had given very little thought as to what sort of young lady he desired.

Lord Jennings shook his head, laughed, and threw back the rest of his whisky, getting to his feet again and setting the glass down on the small table beside him.

"I shall leave you to your reveries," he said with a small bow. "Tell me, when do you hope to meet with Lady Croome again?"

"Tomorrow," Oliver replied without much feeling. "We are to attend Lord and Lady Wellford's evening assembly." His mind was still too clouded with the shock and the strain from what he had just read in the new will, as well as with everything else both he and Lord Jennings had discussed.

"Then I hope you are in better spirits come the morrow, even if the burden is still a heavy one to bear," Lord Jennings finished, throwing a glance of concern over his shoulder. "You shall still gain the rest of your fortune and have a pretty little wife along with it." One shoulder lifted. "It is not an entirely desperate situation."

Oliver did not answer but raised a hand in farewell as Lord Jennings left the room. If the remainder of his father's fortune had not been a significant sum, then of course, Oliver would have simply allowed it to go to this distant cousin, whoever he was, and would have continued with his life as planned. However, without it, he would spend many years doing all he could to make certain that the estate brought in enough funds each year and would be very limited in what he could do to improve it. It was as though his father was attempting to punish him from beyond the grave simply because Oliver had refused to choose a bride when he had been asked.

"I must write to Tabitha," he murmured to himself, rubbing one hand over his eyes and feeling his spirits sink lower than ever before. This was worse than he had ever imagined and, having been in a place of triumph, it was all the worse to know that his plans and his hope of freedom had been shattered in an instant. With a groan, Oliver set down his quill before he had even written a word, a heavy weight on his shoulders that he now feared would never loosen. All was undone, all was at an end. His father, it appeared, had prevailed.

CHAPTER FOUR

Tabitha frowned, recalling the note that she had received from Lord Yarmouth only yesterday. It had been a very strange one indeed, for it seemed to state that all was not well, but without any particular detail as to what it was that troubled him so.

Sighing to herself, Tabitha sat back in her carriage and let her eyes close for a few moments. Having considered all that Lord Jennings had suggested and having seen the way that Lord Yarmouth's face had lit up with a fresh hope when she had stated that she would consider what had been said, there had been contentment deep within her heart when she thought of engaging herself to Lord Yarmouth. It would be a simple way to ensure that he was able to fulfill the demands of his late father's will and would bring no lasting damage to either of them, so long as they were careful.

A small sigh rippled from the corner of her mouth as that same sense of satisfaction filled her once more. Why she had not thought of engaging herself to Lord Yarmouth before, she did not know, but she was grateful that Lord Jennings had seen fit to come up with the suggestion. Why, then, had Lord Yarmouth's note seemed to be so sorrowful? He had stated that there was something he needed to discuss with her as soon as she was next able to meet with him but had not written what such a thing was. There had been a seriousness about his words, a sense of urgency.

Of course, she had replied to him at once, stating that she would have afternoon calls the following afternoon and, thereafter, was attending an evening soiree, but that she would be glad to call upon him whenever he was free to receive her. There had been no response, which had left Tabitha unsure and uncertain as to what was expected of her. Her mind had turned to all manner of things when she wondered what it was he wished to discuss with her, leaving her more concerned for him. Surely something untoward had not occurred? He had seemed so very pleased at her agreement to engage herself to him for a time, but then to have such a happiness stolen away soon afterward seemed to be very strange indeed.

You have a great deal of concern for him.

The thought did not bring her any sort of embarrassment or confusion. Of course, she reasoned, she was concerned for Lord Yarmouth! He had become a very dear friend and was not someone that she was likely to forget about. Over the course of the last few years, they had found a friendship that was unlike anything Tabitha had ever experienced before. Of course, there were those in society who looked down upon them both for such behavior, but Tabitha did not care. As a widow, she was not held to the same stringent requirements as the debutantes and the unmarried young ladies who filled London every Season, and that sense of freedom had bolstered her courage all the more.

The carriage came to a stop, and Tabitha quickly sat up, pressing one hand to the back of her hair to make certain that nothing had been shaken loose from its pins. Thankfully, her curls were still all set in place, and she emerged from the carriage soon afterward before making her way into Lord and Lady Lancaster's townhouse.

"Good evening, Lady Croome," cried Lady Lancaster, holding out both hands to Tabitha as she approached. "I am so very glad you have been able to attend."

Having been briefly acquainted with Lady Lancaster in her debutante year, before either of them had been wed, Tabitha was herself a little glad to see the lady again. There was not a strong friendship between them, but a warm acquaintance, and that was more than satisfactory.

"Good evening, Lady Lancaster," she replied, taking the lady's hands but inclining her head before dropping her hands back to her sides again. "And Lord Lancaster, good evening." This time, she dropped into a correct curtsy, which Lord Lancaster acknowledged and returned with a bow.

"Thank you for joining our little soiree this evening,"

he said with a welcoming smile. "I have heard that you play the pianoforte very well indeed." His eyes were warm as he tilted his head just a fraction. "Perhaps you will be inclined to play for us all later in the evening."

Tabitha laughed, fully aware that his wife had been the one to suggest such a thing. "Perhaps I shall, Lord Lancaster," she replied with a smile of her own. "Thank you again for your invitation to this evening."

"Please." He gestured to the room before her, and Tabitha walked inside without further hesitation. There were already a good number of guests present this evening, but Tabitha gave no thought to any of them. Rather, her eyes searched for Lord Yarmouth, uncertain as to whether or not he would be present this evening. Since he had not replied to her note, she was not certain where he would be. Her gaze snagged on a gentleman she recognized—one Lord Jennings. Her stomach tightened with a sudden tension as he looked back at her, inclining his head but no smile playing around his mouth.

Lord Yarmouth is ill?

Her heart began to race with a desperate fear. Was Lord Yarmouth gravely ill? Was he soon to draw close to death? Perhaps that was the news he wished to impart to her! Perhaps he had received word from one of his doctors and had been forced to face what was now waiting for him. A deep fear began to wind its way up through Tabitha's heart, and she forced herself to make her way towards Lord Jennings, even though she now feared what it was he would say.

"Good evening, Lady Croome."

"Is Lord Yarmouth not here this evening?" Fully aware that she was being rude, Tabitha could only stare into Lord Jennings' face, her heart hammering with a furiousness that stole her breath.

"I believe he intended to be present, given that he accepted the invitation," Lord Jennings replied, his brow furrowing as he studied Tabitha's tight expression. "He has not informed you of his whereabouts this evening?"

"No, he has not," Tabitha replied, one hand reaching up to press against her heart. "I received a note from him stating that there was something of great importance that he wished to discuss with me, but since then, I have not heard from him."

Lord Jennings' brow lowered all the more, sending thick grooves across his forehead. "I see," he replied heavily. "I am sorry for that, Lady Croome, but there is nothing that I can say, for it is not my place to do so. Clearly, the realization of what now faces him is now settling on his shoulders, and it may be that he is struggling to come to terms with it all."

That furious fear that blew like a stormy wind all through Tabitha forced her to speak, tears forming in the corners of her eyes. "Is he unwell?" she whispered, her free hand reaching out to grasp Lord Jennings' arm. "Is he to die?"

Lord Jennings' eyes rounded for a moment, and then he smiled, shaking his head at her. "No, indeed not, my lady," he said calmly. "He is neither unwell nor about to face death. I am sure that his letter to you sounded very grave, but there is nothing that puts Lord Yarmouth in any sort of danger at present." A small, reassuring smile tipped his mouth. "Pray, do not concern yourself with that thought any longer."

Tabitha dropped her head and her hand back to her side, feeling the tight band across her chest immediately release as she took in what Lord Jennings had said. It was not a matter of illness, then. That was a great relief indeed.

"You care very deeply for Lord Yarmouth, do you not?" Lord Jennings murmured, as Tabitha lifted her head to look at him. "I do not think he has anyone else within his acquaintances and friends that hold the same amount of consideration and concern for him as you, Lady Croome."

Wondering if this was to be a compliment, Tabitha smiled sweetly but looked away. "We are very dear friends," she said, wondering at this strange sense of nervousness that rose within her chest as she spoke. "It is quite right that I should be thus concerned."

"Of course, of course," Lord Jennings replied with a small smile of his own. "I am sure that Lord Yarmouth greatly appreciates your friendship, Lady Croome. Would that I had someone such as you to take such great pains over me!"

Tabitha glanced back at him but saw that his words were genuine. With another smile, she thanked him for his reassurance, begged his apology for behaving in such a manner—which he immediately dismissed—and then moved away to allow him to speak to other guests whilst she forced herself to do the same.

Conversations abounded, but Tabitha paid them all

very little attention. Yes, she did what was required, speaking to the other guests with interest and consideration but finding no enjoyment in anything that was said. Rather, she found her thoughts turning, again and again, to Lord Yarmouth. Just where was he, and what was it he wanted to talk to her about?

~

"THANK you for that wonderful performance, Lady Croome."

Rising quickly from the pianoforte and praying that she would not be called upon again to play, Tabitha made her way from the instrument to a quiet corner of the room, grateful when Lady Lancaster herself rose to take her turn. She had managed to play a few pieces quite well and had been gratified when the rest of the guests applauded politely, but her mind had struggled to fix itself to the music she usually knew so well, continuing to pull itself back to Lord Yarmouth. He had not appeared this evening, and she had found herself growing steadily more downhearted and anxious as the evening progressed. As she sat down quietly, part of her wondered whether or not she ought to take a carriage to his townhouse during afternoon calls tomorrow, simply to force her way into his presence and to demand to know what concerned him, given just how much difficulty it was causing her! But then she pushed the idea from her mind, not wishing to force Lord Yarmouth into speaking with her if he was not ready to do so.

"And that concludes our performances for the

evening!" Lord Lancaster exclaimed as his wife came to join him. "Thank you all for attending. If you wish to remain, there will be card tables set up and refreshments brought. Otherwise, allow us both to wish you all a good evening."

Tabitha did not immediately move from her chair, not quite certain what was best to do. She did not want to be rude and depart before others did, but at the same time, there was no enjoyment to be found here this evening. Instead, she would be faced with frustration and upset, her mind still wondering about Lord Yarmouth whilst she forced herself to play the part of someone enjoying the evening very much indeed.

A sudden ripple of surprise caught her attention, and she lifted her eyes to where Lord and Lady Lancaster were standing, noting how other guests were turning to each other and speaking quietly as though there was something there that they wanted to remark upon but did not want to be overheard.

"Nonsense!" Lord Lancaster boomed, his voice filling the room. "You must stay. We shall play cards and the like and, if that does not persuade you, then surely the thought of the very best French brandy will do!"

Tabitha's breath caught as she saw who the gentleman was speaking to. Lord Yarmouth had evidently come into the room without her being aware of it and was now standing close to Lord and Lady Lancaster, a look of apology written all over his face.

She rose before immediately sitting down again. It would not do for her to make her way directly towards Lord Yarmouth, not in front of the other guests. That was how rumors began, and she did not need any additional whispers at present. Instead, Tabitha forced herself to remain seated, although her eyes fixed themselves to Lord Yarmouth as he spoke first to one guest and then to another. Grateful that she was in a quiet corner of the room and, therefore, not really noticed by the other guests, Tabitha allowed herself to study Lord Yarmouth as he made his way from one conversation to the next. He appeared, outwardly, to be in excellent spirits, for he smiled often, laughed on occasion, and otherwise seemed to be enjoying the company that surrounded him. However, she noted quickly that the brightness of his smile did not reach his eyes and that, whenever someone else spoke, the contented look disappeared from his face almost at once, replaced with a look of severity that he was continually forced to wipe away.

Finally, he came towards her, and Tabitha had to resist the urge to throw herself to her feet and rush towards him, such was her angst. Instead, she lifted her face to greet him but did not otherwise rise. Lord Yarmouth reached out one hand and, a little confused, Tabitha gave it to him at once. Leaning over it, he pressed his lips to the back of her hand in a fervent manner, sending heat spiraling up into her face.

"Whatever are you doing, Yarmouth?" she hissed, yanking her hand away as he sat down heavily beside her. "Do you want the *ton* to whisper about us?" She had not meant to speak so severely, but his actions had embarrassed her somewhat and she did not want him to behave inappropriately. Was he in his cups?

"Forgive me, Tabitha," Lord Yarmouth said, his shoulders slumping and no trace of a smile on his face now. "Forgive me for not returning your letter, for leaving you to wonder what it is that I meant." He gestured towards Lord Jennings. "He spoke to me as I entered, telling me that you had been gravely concerned for me."

"Of course I have been," Tabitha replied, finding herself growing a little frustrated with his manner. "You write to me that there is something of importance that you must discuss with me, only to then refuse to reply to my note! For heavens' sake, Yarmouth, I feared you might be dying!" Her voice, she realized, had become a little too loud, and she forced herself to speak quietly once more, refusing to allow her worry to take hold of her. "You are late this evening, however, which is not at all like you. Why do you not tell me what has happened?" Her hand reached across to settle on his arm in what she hoped was a surreptitious manner. She did not want anyone from the *ton* to start whispering about what they had seen of her and Lord Yarmouth. "What is troubling you, Yarmouth?"

Lord Yarmouth let out a long breath, looked down at her hand, and then raised his eyes to hers. There was despair written in his eyes that Tabitha had never seen before, making her swallow hard with the fear of what might soon be revealed.

"Another will was found," he said hoarsely, making Tabitha's eyes flare wide with astonishment. "The solicitor believes it is the last of my father's many, *many* wills, for it was written and signed the day before he departed this earth."

"I see," Tabitha murmured, lifting her hand back to her lap and trying her best to keep her expression entirely neutral. "And what did this will say?"

A heavy sigh tore from his lips. "That I must be *wed* by the end of the six months," he said, closing his eyes. "Not only engaged but wed."

For a few moments, Tabitha did not know what to say. Was he now stating that he wished her to marry him? She had never once considered such a thing, for Lord Yarmouth was nothing more than a friend, and she had told herself repeatedly that she did not wish to give up her freedom as yet. But if he needed her to do so, if he was to ask her to become his wife, then what would she say?

You would say yes.

The quiet voice in her head stunned her, and her breath hitched as Lord Yarmouth lifted his gaze to hers, his expression miserable.

"I have tried to think of what I can do to escape this judgment," he said heavily. "I have done my utmost to consider what can be done in order to revert back to the previous will, but there is nothing available to me that would be of any particular use. Therefore, I have no other choice."

"You—you must marry," Tabitha whispered as Lord Yarmouth nodded, his eyes squeezing closed and one hand curling into a fist in obvious frustration. "That must be a very difficult circumstance to consider."

Lord Yarmouth let out another long breath and looked at her again. "It is more than difficult," he said hoarsely. "It is impossible. You know that I have never wanted to be forced into matrimony. I have wanted to make such a decision in my own time, rather than do as is expected of me. And yet, given the vast amount of money that my father has kept from me in his will, it seems now that I must do as he demanded."

"Must you truly do so?" Tabitha asked gently, wishing she could say more and finding her own reaction to such news overwhelming. "Is there not a way where you might forge your own path and leave the money to fall to your relative?" She held his gaze, but Lord Yarmouth closed his eyes and looked away, dropping his head forward for a moment.

"I need the remainder of my father's wealth to keep the estate in a good state," he told her sadly. "Else, I shall be struggling for many years, with no reassurance that I shall be able to succeed."

"I see." Tabitha drew in a long breath, finding herself all the more willing to accept Lord Yarmouth's hand in marriage. It would be a marriage of friendship, of course, but that was something that she could find happiness in. The idea of being his wife did not throw her away from him at once, and nor did it make her want to run from him, want to escape from what now faced him. Rather, she found herself almost pleased with the idea, knowing that Lord Yarmouth would be the sort of husband who would grant her the freedom she so obviously desired, given that he would trust her to be loyal to him. "Then, I understand what you must do."

Lord Yarmouth's head lifted. "Do you?" he asked, reaching out to put one hand over hers despite the number of guests about them. "I confess I have been struggling with the prospect for many hours. I could not even bring myself to reply to you, Tabitha, which I know was wrong of me given the worry that must have swamped you." With a wry smile, he withdrew his hand. "Lord Jennings said that you would be an excellent judge of character, and I do not think he is wrong."

Tabitha frowned, not quite certain what he meant. "An excellent judge of character?"

"Indeed," Lord Yarmouth replied quickly. "You know those within the *ton,* and you are, much to my gratitude, a very dear friend of mine. If you are still willing, then I should be very glad indeed of your assistance in this matter."

Tabitha's mouth opened and then closed again without a single word coming from it. She had been mistaken, then. He was not to ask her to marry him. Rather, it seemed, he was asking for her help in finding him a bride.

"But it will need to be soon," Lord Yarmouth said, shaking his head to himself. "I will need to court them and, if they are suitable, become engaged, and thereafter make all the arrangements." His eyes sought hers and held her fast, but Tabitha could not smile at him, could not even bring herself to nod. "You are very kind, dear friend. I am truly grateful for your help."

"But of course," Tabitha managed to say, her throat aching. "I would be very glad indeed to help you find a suitable match. When shall we begin?"

Lord Yarmouth sat back in his chair and gestured to the other guests around them. "This evening?" he suggested, although there was no happiness in his expression but a set resolution that Tabitha knew hid a great many emotions. "There must be some here this evening that you might consider for me!"

Tabitha's smile was tight, but she dragged her eyes away from him and looked out across the crowd. "I am sure there are," she found herself saying, aware of the dull ache in her heart and wondering at it. "Just allow me a moment to consider."

"But of course."

Tabitha's eyes roved across the room but, try as she might, she could not seem to fix her gaze on anyone in particular. Giving herself a slight shake, she tried her utmost to set her mind to the task, but such was the business of her mind, her thoughts trying to settle themselves into a calming pattern, that she simply could not.

"I do not think there is anyone here I would recommend," she said briskly, looking back at Lord Yarmouth, who looked a little astonished at her decision. "At least, not at present."

"Oh?"

She shrugged. "Well, I must give time to my considerations, Yarmouth. I must think of your character and, in light of that, think of the ladies of my acquaintance to see which I might suggest to you." It was an excellent excuse, she thought to herself, seeing him nod slowly, and one that was quite true. She *would* have to give it greater consideration but, additionally, would require time to allow what he had told her to settle into her mind and heart. It was not that she was at all saddened that she would not be able to engage herself to him, but rather that it had all come as something of a surprise. That was all it was, she told herself firmly, gazing around the room. She was quite sure that, come the morrow, she would be back to her usual temperament and more than able to assist Lord Yarmouth in finding a suitable bride.

CHAPTER FIVE

The soiree had gone as well as Oliver had expected, although he had been very late in arriving. Thankfully, Lord Lancaster had not seemed much put out, and Lady Lancaster had been delighted with the fact that his tardiness had brought something of a stir to her guests. No one had departed from the house for some hours after his arrival, and the evening had gone on for hours, with cards, music, and much laughter and conversation. The sun had already begun to rise by the time Oliver had returned home, but he had not thought poorly of himself for remaining at the Lancaster soiree for so long. It had been something of a salve to his wounds, a few hours of levity instead of the heaviness that hung over his heart. And even Lady Croome had taken his news well, agreeing without hesitation to securing him a suitable match.

After having slept late and taken an even later breakfast, Oliver was now enjoying a quiet afternoon, although he was eagerly anticipating the arrival of Lady Croome.

She had written to him earlier that day—the note received when he was asleep—stating that she would call upon him in the early afternoon. Lord Jennings was also to be present, and thus, there would be no cause for even the suggestion of impropriety. Oliver was looking forward to seeing her, a little surprised at his own anticipation but finding that, in pulling himself from his struggles, he had found a little happiness once more. It would not last long, given that he would soon have to become quite serious about finding himself a bride, with all the requirements of courtship and the like, but for the next few days at least, he could continue with the Season as he wished. Lady Croome and Lord Jennings would be excellent company, and he would refuse to give into the frustrations and the anger that still boiled within him. He had spent two days moping, miserable and upset, but in the end had told himself that he had no other choice but to accept his new circumstances and make the best of them. And making the best of them meant having Lady Croome assist him in selecting the most appropriate lady from amongst the *beau monde.*

Sighing to himself, Oliver ran one hand through his hair and leaned back in his chair. When he had spoken to Lady Croome last evening, he had not expected her to be as shocked and astonished as she had appeared. Instead, he had expected relief to be evidenced on her face, a slumping of her shoulders, a long sigh escaping from her as she realized she would not have to do what he had asked of her. But instead, she had stared at him with wide eyes, before turning her head away, clearly unsure about what she ought to do or say in response. It was, of course, just that she cared deeply for him as one friend to another, but still, he had been touched by her reaction. And the fact that she had so willingly agreed to help him had made things all the more hopeful.

"Good afternoon, Yarmouth."

Lord Jennings strolled into the room and spoke a greeting before the butler could even introduce him. "You look a little tired this afternoon."

"As do you," Oliver retorted as Lord Jennings grinned. "I presume, given that you were just as late as I in departing, that you had an enjoyable time last evening?"

"I did," Lord Jennings replied, folding himself into a chair. "Although I think Lady Croome was worried about you."

"Oh?" Oliver rose to fetch both himself and Lord Jennings a brandy, ringing the bell to call for the butler as he did so. "What was she concerned about?"

Lord Jennings rolled his eyes and laughed as Oliver handed him his glass. "She was concerned for *you*, Yarmouth," he said with an exasperated sigh. "Do you not yet understand? You wrote her a note, but when she replied, you did not respond to her. Therefore, her mind was whirling with all manner of possibilities as to what might have occurred to make you write such words to her."

"I see," Oliver replied, frowning just a little. The butler came into the room at Oliver's summons, and Oliver quickly reminded him that a tea tray was to be prepared and thereafter, sent up once Lady Croome had arrived. Once the butler had gone, Oliver resumed his conversation with Lord Jennings, seeing how his friend was watching him with a careful eye.

"I am sorry I did not write to her," Oliver said, aware that he should be making his apology to Lady Croome herself rather than to Lord Jennings. "I was...rather lost."

"I quite understand," Lord Jennings replied firmly. "But my question remains—did you speak to Lady Croome thereafter? Did you tell her all that had occurred?"

"I did," Oliver said, still surprised at Lord Jennings' curious expression and wondering why he appeared so interested in Lady Croome. "And she was quite wonderful about it all."

Lord Jennings nodded slowly, lifting his glass to his mouth for a sip before he continued. "I see," he remarked, tilting his head. "She has agreed to assist you, then?"

"But of course!" Oliver exclaimed, not wanting Lord Jennings to have a poor impression of the lady. "She was more than willing. She was, in fact, about to give me her opinion on some of the other guests there last evening, given that there were more than a few eligible ladies, but in the end, she did not quite manage to do so." Seeing Lord Jennings' lifted brow, Oliver waved a hand in exasperation. "She has to consider each of the ladies in light of what she knows about me," he continued calmly. "It was too much to ask her to do it almost immediately."

Lord Jennings nodded slowly. "I quite understand," he said, but still, the look of curiosity lingered on his face. "She was, as you know, quite upset and concerned for you, Yarmouth. It may have been that the relief of knowing you were not unwell or the like might have overcome her somewhat."

Thinking that Lord Jennings was, for whatever reason, quite determined to make him feel as guilty as possible for his lack of consideration towards Lady Croome, Oliver threw up his hands. "Yes, I am aware that she was very concerned for me, Lord Jennings," he said in exasperation. "I shall apologize to her for my lack of response the very moment she arrives."

Saying nothing, Lord Jennings took a sip of his brandy and continued to observe Oliver thoughtfully, which only irritated him all the more. Choosing to remain silent also instead of giving in to the urge to defend himself thoroughly, Oliver drank his brandy and sat back in his chair, glowering somewhat. Lord Jennings looked quite contented, however, smiling to himself and shaking his head as though something amused him. It was on the tip of Oliver's tongue to ask him what it was, but he then bit down hard, refusing to allow himself to do so. Lord Jennings would only be delighted that he had irritated Oliver enough to force him to ask such a question, and he did not want to give his friend any such satisfaction.

Mercifully, the door soon opened to reveal Lady Croome, who appeared just as lovely as he had ever seen her. Her cheeks were pink, her blue eyes sparkling like the sunshine dancing off the water, and a few dark curls danced about her temples, framing her face beautifully.

"Good afternoon, Lady Croome," Oliver said, quickly rising from his chair to bow as Lord Jennings did the same. "You look very well this morning."

"I walked from the house," Lady Croome declared, clearly delighted with her exertion. "The day was so very fine that I thought it would be a waste to take the carriage or to hail a hackney."

Lord Jennings smiled at her and gestured to a chair, and Lady Croome immediately sat down, perhaps a little tired from her walk.

"Then might I say it looks as though it has done you a world of good," Lord Jennings said as Oliver made his way towards them both, removing himself from his seat in the corner of the room. "You appear much cheered this morning, given the anxiety that bound you last evening." One hard glance was sent towards Oliver at this remark, but Oliver ignored it quickly, sitting himself down in a chair adjacent to Lady Croome's. She smiled at him but said nothing, her gaze darting back to Lord Jennings for just a moment.

"Ah!" Oliver exclaimed as a scratch came at the door. "Your tea tray, Lady Croome!"

"Wonderful, I thank you," Lady Croome replied, looking at the tray of refreshments with bright eyes. "I am quite famished, even though it has not been too long since luncheon!"

"Then please," Oliver said grandly, "do not hold back on our account, Lady Croome." He lifted one eyebrow in the direction of Lord Jennings in an attempt to state that Lady Croome, it seemed, was in quite good spirits and certainly not injured in any way by his lack of response to her note. Lord Jennings merely smiled and turned his head away, leaving Lady Croome to look from one to the other, her forehead beginning to wrinkle in confusion.

Seeing this, Oliver spread his hands. "It is only that Lord Jennings and I were discussing how things were last evening," he said by way of explanation. "That is all."

"I see," Lady Croome murmured, picking up her teacup and taking a sip. "Then you will be glad to know, Lord Yarmouth, that I have at least three young ladies that I think worthy enough to suggest to you."

Oliver blinked in surprise, missing the broad grin that spread across Lord Jennings's face. "Indeed," he murmured. "So soon."

She shrugged. "I am well acquainted with many within the *beau monde*," she reminded him. "I had some time this morning to consider things, and during my considerations, the names of three young ladies, in particular, came to mind. I am quite certain that they will all be at Hyde Park this afternoon. Where, of course, we must go if you are to observe them from afar and, if you like any of them in particular, then we shall continue with introductions. That is," she finished, with a quick smile, "if you are not acquainted with them already!"

"What are their names?" Oliver asked, finding nothing but a sense of disappointment clouding his soul as though he had wanted Lady Croome to appear at the house without any great enthusiasm to do as he had asked, which was quite a foolish thought in itself. "Are their fathers all titled? Do they have—"

"Let us take one thing at a time," Lady Croome interrupted, laughing. "Else, you shall do nothing but ask me questions and may even refuse to look upon them, which certainly will not do."

Oliver attempted to look offended. "I shall do nothing

of the sort!" he declared, eyeing her. "What questions do you think I might ask that would then make me turn away from them?"

A coy smile spread across Lady Croome's face. "You think that I do not know you as well as I do?" she asked with a quiet laugh. "Do you think that I do not know that, should a lady be the second daughter of a titled gentleman, who therefore would be granted a smaller dowry, that you would not look down upon such a connection?" She laughed as Oliver dropped his head, feeling a flush burn up his neck and into his face. "You may not have ever acknowledged such a thing out loud, but I know still that those particular desires linger on within your heart."

Oliver did not know what to say. It was true that he had never once expressed that particular suggestion to either Lord Jennings or to Lady Croome, but somehow, she already knew that about him. It was a rather discomfiting sensation, and, as he shot her a glance, he felt his flush burn all the hotter as she laughed again.

"Well, this is very interesting, indeed!" Lord Jennings exclaimed, rising from his chair and coming towards Oliver, standing behind him. "Tell me, Lady Croome. If Lord Yarmouth were to choose a lady based solely on the color of her hair and the shade of her eyes, then what sort of lady might he choose?"

No, Oliver thought to himself, holding his head up a little more as he looked back at Lady Croome, quite certain that he had the victory here. *There is no feasible way for her to ever gain such knowledge. I am certain of it.*

For a moment, it looked as though Lady Croome was entirely uncertain about her answer, for she studied

Oliver with that familiar gaze, looking into his face as if she might find the answer there.

And then, she grinned.

Oliver's heart sank.

"I think that, should Lord Yarmouth have a choice before him such as the one you have described, Lord Jennings, he would settle on a lady with fair tresses that gleam gold in the sun." Her eyes danced with merriment as Oliver stared fixedly at her, his astonishment growing with every moment. "And he would prefer that a lady have green eyes of some description. Although he would accept brown eyes, similar to his own."

Oliver shook his head in astonishment, unable to join in the laughter that came from both Lady Croome and Lord Jennings. "Quite how you know such a thing about me, I cannot even begin to imagine," he said as Lady Croome giggled, her eyes sparkling.

"Does that mean that she is correct, then?" Lord Jennings asked, grinning broadly as he resumed his seat. "You cannot deny the truth, simply to save face!"

Closing his eyes, Oliver let out a long breath. "Yes, indeed, it is all just as she says," he replied with a shake of his head. "It is almost frightening to hear my innermost thoughts spoken aloud by another!"

"It merely shows the depths of our friendship," Lady Croome replied, picking up her teacup again. "But once we are finished with our time here, I should like very much to go to Hyde Park with you both in the hope of pointing out these young ladies, should they be present." She smiled at him. "Otherwise, the ball this evening should be adequate, although I am sure you should like to be aware of them first before you ask them to dance."

Oliver swallowed hard, feeling a strange reluctance building up within him. He did not want to have these young women pointed out to him. He did not want to have to acquaint himself with them or ask them to dance. It was all becoming a little too overwhelming, making him realize that he might very well find himself courting a lady by this time next week. A lady who could, in three or four short weeks, become his betrothed. And who, a month thereafter, would become his wife.

"Hyde Park sounds like a capital idea!" Lord Jennings boomed as Oliver fought to keep his composure. "Although, do have as much tea as you wish, Lady Croome, before we set out." He chuckled, and Oliver frowned. "Although, I do not think it will be you who requires sustaining!"

"I am quite all right," Oliver snapped, surprising both Lord Jennings and Lady Croome. "Shall we set out?" He did not wait for their answer but rose to his feet and walked from the room, leaving Lady Croome and Lord Jennings to follow. The fast beating of his heart and the sweat that broke out on his brow betrayed a gentleman rather overwhelmed with emotion, but it was not something he would speak of to anyone. Not even Lady Croome.

"If she knows me as well as she states, then surely she will already know of my feelings on this matter," he muttered to himself, striding towards the front door, his brows low over his eyes as his jaw set. How he wished he could have some of the same glee that Lady Croome and

Lord Jennings exhibited so easily! But try as he might, Oliver could feel nothing but frustration, distress, and pain. This afternoon would not be a pleasant one, no matter how much he wished it otherwise.

"You are not going to leave without us, I hope?"

He stopped at the front door, turning to see Lady Croome coming after him.

"Lord Jennings will be but a moment," she said, settling one hand on his arm as she came to stand in front of him. There was no laughter in her expression now, only concern. "Something is troubling you, is it not?"

Letting out his breath slowly, Oliver closed his eyes. "It is difficult to imagine myself betrothed within only a few weeks," he said, admitting aloud the fears in his heart. "And then to be wed only a month after that."

Her smile was gentle and filled with understanding. "I quite understand," she told him, and there was truth within her words. "My first Season, I still recall my father telling me that I would be wed within a month. I had only a few months in London and, within that time, was given an opportunity to simply prepare myself for being a bride. It came as something of a shock to be told such a thing, but there was nothing for me to do but accept."

Oliver felt the tension begin to leave his frame, looking down at Lady Croome and finding that her quiet words had broken the chain that had been tight across his chest. "You very rarely speak of your father."

"There is no need to do so," she replied with a lightness that he did not truly believe. "Now that I am an independent widow, he has no need to consider me. That was his primary goal, I believe." Her eyes clouded for a moment. "To remove responsibility from himself, so that he would not have to consider me any further."

This brought a spark of anger to Oliver's heart, and he placed his hand over hers. "That is not the way of a gentleman."

"But it is the way of my father," Lady Croome replied, looking up at him with a rueful smile. "Fathers are strange creatures, Lord Yarmouth. They make strange requests of us, demand that we do what they wish, and think of consequences to face us when we do not do as they wish."

Fully aware that she was speaking of not only her own father but also of his, Oliver could only grunt in response. Lady Croome knew all too well the difficulties that had faced him when it came to his father, and he realized now that she could well understand the struggles his own heart was facing, given that she had been forced into matrimony herself.

"But we must face what is given us with a strong determination to make the best of it," Lady Croome finished, her gaze still fixed and steady. "For if we do not, then everything will seem dark and filled with misery. And what will become of our hearts then?"

Oliver lifted her hand to his lips and kissed the back of it. "You are always so very kind, Tabitha," he told her, honestly. "Your words bring comfort to my heart and quietness to my discontented spirit."

"I did not mean to tease you," she said, now appearing to be a trifle anxious. "It was only in—"

"There is nothing that you need concern yourself with," he interrupted, letting her hand go as the sound of

Lord Jennings' footsteps began to hurry towards them. "You are my dearest friend, Lady Croome, and I am truly grateful for your guidance and for your sweet words of comfort." With a smile, he settled his shoulders and drew in a long breath. "Very well. To Hyde Park we shall go."

Lady Croome smiled up at him. "With determination in our hearts?"

"With determination and intent," he said with a small bow. "And a promise that I shall consider each and every lady with great care, Tabitha, so that you cannot find fault with me."

For a moment, it seemed as though a shadow fell across Lady Croome's face, but it was gone seconds later.

"Then let us go," she said cheerfully, just as Lord Jennings joined them. "Let us see just what you make of each lady I have chosen!" Her eyes twinkled as she smiled up at him. "But have no fear. If you find legitimate fault with them, Lord Yarmouth, then I have every intention of settling more before your eyes!"

"I am grateful," Oliver replied, as Lord Jennings chuckled quietly. "Can I lead you to the carriage, my lady?" He gave her an overdone bow, and Lady Croome laughed before giving him her hand. It was in better spirits that Oliver led her to his waiting carriage, thinking quietly to himself that Lady Croome was truly the best of ladies. There was none like her, and, indeed, he was truly grateful for all that she offered him.

CHAPTER SIX

Their visit to Hyde Park had not gone as well as Tabitha had hoped. There had only been two of the ladies present, and when she had pointed each one out to Lord Yarmouth, he had not made any expression of delight at her suggestions. Both the young ladies had been pretty, from good families, and with a decent dowry; as far as Tabitha was concerned, they would have suited him very well indeed. But, for whatever reason, he had wrinkled his nose and shaken his head—to the point that Tabitha herself had wanted to shake him in frustration! Did he not know just how difficult it had been for her to even *consider* some of these young ladies? Had he any understanding of the trouble that had tormented her soul when she had thought of what he had asked her to do?

Of course, she reasoned, he had no knowledge of it whatsoever, and given that she herself had no real understanding as to why she felt such a way when it was a very reasonable and understandable request that he had made, it was better that he did not know of her own emotions on the subject either.

"You are certain that these three young ladies are wise choices for Lord Yarmouth?"

Tabitha looked at her friend. "I should think so," she said as Lady Ashbrook pursed her lips thoughtfully. "Unless there is something about their character that I am not aware of as yet?"

Lady Ashbrook frowned, but then shook her head. "No, there is nothing that comes to my mind," she said quietly, making Tabitha wonder why she had even questioned Tabitha's choice in the first place. "I suppose, it is only that I know so little of Lord Yarmouth's preferences and considerations that I ask. But," she continued, with a wry smile, "I suppose that is why he asked you to be involved."

"Precisely," Tabitha replied, ignoring the strange tightness that took hold of her heart for a moment. "Miss Bartlett is the daughter of a viscount, Lady Marina is the daughter of an earl, as is Lady Emma. I am sure that these young ladies are more than suitable, although Lady Emma does have a few airs and graces that might be a trifle irritating."

Lady Ashbrook chuckled. "Lady Emma is the daughter of the Earl of Blackmore, is she not?" she asked, as Tabitha nodded. "Then she takes after her mother, who is well known to be rather proud of her marriage to the earl. I believe she was nothing more than the daughter of a viscount, who did very well in her marriage. She has not forgotten it since the day she became engaged!"

Tabitha tried to laugh, but the sound stuck in her throat. Why was she finding it so very difficult to place a young lady in front of Lord Yarmouth? What was it that troubled her so? She could not place precisely what it was, but it grew with force every time Lord Yarmouth and his proposed engagement came to her mind.

"There he is!" Lady Ashbrook exclaimed, grasping Tabitha's arm tightly. "There! Come now, you must make the first of the introductions, for I confess that I am eager indeed to see what he makes of her."

Forcing a smile to her face, Tabitha allowed Lady Ashbrook to lead her towards Lord Yarmouth, smiling at him as he turned to face her. Lord Jennings, who seemed to be Lord Yarmouth's constant companion at present, greeted them both warmly and then looked at Tabitha expectantly. At this, she could not help but smile. It seemed as though the reason Lord Jennings was almost always in Lord Yarmouth's company was solely because, like Lady Ashbrook, he wanted to see just what Lord Yarmouth would make of her suggestions.

"It seems I am to have a captive audience this evening," Lord Yarmouth said with what appeared to be a grimace. "Lord Jennings is very excited to know just which of the ladies present this evening you are to recommend, Lady Croome."

"Is that so?" Tabitha remarked, arching one eyebrow as she looked back at Lord Jennings, who did nothing but grin. "Then mayhap it is because he also is seeking a bride and wishes very much to know the ladies I think most suitable, in the hope that, should you refuse them, he might then consider them." Her smile spread as Lord

Jennings flushed and dropped his gaze, his hands tight behind his back as he stammered that it was not so, making the others laugh. Tabitha could not help but join in, feeling pleased that they were able to tease Lord Jennings instead of him focusing solely on Lord Yarmouth's present circumstances.

"In all seriousness, however," Lord Yarmouth said once the smiles had faded, "I should like to know the lady you intend to introduce me to first."

"That I shall not do," Tabitha told him as his eyes flared wide. "For you shall do as you did this afternoon— look at her and decide that she shall *not* do. Thus, if you will attend with me, I shall make certain to introduce you to the lady. Thereafter, you will seek to dance with her, although I cannot be certain that she will have any remaining spaces."

Lord Yarmouth looked a little impressed. "Then she is well known in the *beau monde*?" he asked as Tabitha lifted one shoulder. "Had I perhaps been eager to spend more time in society and to make introductions of my own, then mayhap I would know her."

"Mayhap you already do," Tabitha told him, taking his arm and seeing Lady Ashbrook and Lord Jennings coming after them. "I shall not make the introduction obvious, of course, but you *must* converse with her and dance at least once before you can make any sort of judgment."

Lord Yarmouth nodded firmly, his jaw set and no expression of delight or even enjoyment on his face.

"And you must *try* to look a little pleased when you are introduced," Tabitha insisted, unable to hide her smile. "At present, you appear to be greatly worried about what is to come."

"Perhaps I am," he replied, making her smile fade in an instant. "It is a very odd situation, Tabitha. I always hoped that I should one day find a lady whose presence was something I could not turn from. I wanted to find myself thinking of her often, to know that there was even an interest there before I would even consider courtship."

Tabitha smiled gently, appreciating his words and his intentions. "That may still be the case," she suggested tentatively. "Just because a match might be hurried, might be necessary, does not mean that you shall not have an interest as you speak of." Her heart squeezed painfully, but she brushed the feeling aside in a moment. "You might discover yourself quite taken with Lady Emma."

Blinking rapidly, Lord Yarmouth looked down at her with a knitted brow. "Lady Emma?" he repeated. "The daughter of the Earl of Blackmore?"

"Precisely," Tabitha replied, grateful that he had not instantly refused to meet with the lady. "You are acquainted with her already?"

He shook his head. "I am not," he said slowly. "But I have heard of her."

Tabitha dared not ask what specifically he had heard of the lady, choosing instead to remain quiet as they approached. Lady Emma was resplendent in a gown of gentle lavender, her hair cascading down from where it was pinned to the back of her head. She was speaking with animation to someone that Tabitha could not, as yet, identify, but Tabitha noted with interest that Lady

Emma's gaze flickered towards them and then lingered on Lord Yarmouth for a moment or two.

"Good evening, Lady Emma," Tabitha said quickly when there came a moment of silence in the lady's conversation. "I do hope you will recall me? We were introduced some time ago." She smiled warmly at the lady, and, after a moment, the smile was returned.

"But of course, Lady Croome," came the reply as the lady glanced over her shoulder. "I believe my mother introduced us? She is present this evening and standing just there." Her eyes lit up, and she smiled, looking towards Lord Yarmouth as she spoke. "Just so that you do not think I am entirely without decorum!"

"I should not think that at all," Tabitha replied quickly, glancing up at Lord Yarmouth, who was, she noticed, neither smiling nor frowning. In fact, he appeared a little bored with the conversation at present, although he did not make any attempt to turn away.

"Might I present my dear friend, the Earl of Yarmouth," Tabitha said quickly, noting the flicker of curiosity in Lady Emma's blue eyes. "Lord Yarmouth, this is Lady Emma, daughter to Lord Blackmore."

Immediately, Lord Yarmouth dropped into a bow, and Lady Emma curtsied beautifully. Tabitha smiled as they both rose, praying that Lord Yarmouth would do as she had asked him and completely ignoring the way her heart squeezed painfully at the look on Lady Emma's face. It was quite clear that *she*, at the very least, was interested in furthering this particular acquaintance, although Lord Yarmouth himself did not appear to be so. There was no smile on his face, no gleam of interest in his eye, and when he rose from his bow, he appeared to be less than willing to even make conversation!

"It is a very pleasant evening, is it not?" Lady Emma asked, looking directly towards Lord Yarmouth, who cleared his throat in a very gruff manner. "You are enjoying it, I hope?" The question was not directed towards Tabitha but rather to Lord Yarmouth, who did not appear to notice that it was to him that she spoke. A little frustrated, Tabitha was forced to nudge him in the ribs with her elbow as she gesticulated, hoping that it would be enough to remove him from whatever state he was in.

"It is *wonderful!*" she declared, throwing up her hands and managing to prod Lord Yarmouth in the meantime. "Do you not think so, Lord Yarmouth?"

Again, Lord Yarmouth cleared his throat, looking at her with evident frustration, but Tabitha instead ignored him, turning her attention back to Lady Emma, who was now watching Lord Yarmouth with a bemused expression on her face.

"Indeed, it has been an excellent evening thus far," Lord Yarmouth said eventually, his voice gruff. "I dare not even consider whether or not you are free to accept a dance from me later this evening, Lady Emma, for I am quite sure that your card will already be filled to the brim." He inclined his head as if to depart, but Lady Emma was much too quick for him.

"Indeed not!" she cried, snatching the dance card from her arm and immediately thrusting it in his direction. "My dance card is not *quite* full, Lord Yarmouth, although I expect it shall be very soon." Her eyes fastened to his, and Tabitha felt her own heart sink to the floor, fully aware that Lady Emma was already quite enchanted with Lord Yarmouth, clearly aware of his title and his eligibility. "Please," Lady Emma continued as Lord Yarmouth took the dance card from her, "choose whichever you wish. I should be very glad indeed to dance with you, Lord Yarmouth. Thank you for your interest in doing so."

Tabitha could tell from the way that Lord Yarmouth's jaw set that he did not feel much interest in dancing with the lady but was doing so simply to make certain that he fulfilled what he had promised to Tabitha. Quite what it was about Lady Emma that he disliked, Tabitha could not even guess what it might be. Lady Emma was bright, charming, and very eligible, with an excellent dowry and a beauty about her that many ladies of the *ton* envied greatly. What was wrong with the fellow that he could consider her to be entirely without merit when it came to his own marriage?

"The quadrille," Lord Yarmouth said, inclining his head as he handed the card back to Lady Emma. "I do hope that will satisfy you, Lady Emma?"

Rather surprised to see the flare of disappointment in Lady Emma's eyes, Tabitha looked from one to the other as Lady Emma accepted the card back and Lord Yarmouth finally managed to smile. Was something the matter?

"Wonderful, I thank you," Lady Emma replied with a quick curtsy. "Ah, now if you will both excuse me, I am to dance now with Lord Smythe, and I can see him approaching. Good evening."

She did not wait for either Tabitha or Lord Yarmouth to bid her good evening but made her way directly past them and towards another gentleman, whom Tabitha took to be Lord Smythe. The way he looked at Lady Emma was entirely different to the look of disinterest that Lord Yarmouth had shown and, despite her own frustration, Tabitha could not help but feel a small pinch of relief. Checking herself, she turned back to Lord Yarmouth, who was grimacing as though he had just eaten something most distasteful.

"Whatever is the matter, Lord Yarmouth?" she asked, aware that her relief came from the fact that Lord Yarmouth did not seem to be inclined towards Lady Emma but knowing all too well that such feelings were *not* to be entertained. They made very little sense even to her, and she was not going to permit them to take hold of her. She had been asked to do something of importance for Lord Yarmouth, and she was determined to do as he had asked, despite her own strange feelings on the subject.

"What do you mean?" he asked, turning back to where Lady Ashbrook and Lord Jennings were watching, seeing matching expressions of disappointment in their eyes. "I did as you asked."

"You did very little!" Tabitha retorted as their two friends came to join them. "Is there something about Lady Emma that you dislike?"

Lord Jennings rolled his eyes. "You did not appear to be particularly interested in her, Yarmouth. You certainly could have made more of an effort to encourage her interest."

"Although I think her interest is already fixed, that being said," Lady Ashbrook added, looking at Tabitha as she spoke rather than at Lord Yarmouth. "Do you not think so, Lady Croome?"

Tabitha opened her mouth to answer, only for Lord Yarmouth to let out a hiss of breath and turn away from them in frustration. Watching with great astonishment, Tabitha waited for him to return, seeing how he took a few steps away and then came back to them all.

"That is precisely my concern, do you not see?" he asked, clearly irritated. "Lady Emma is one of the young ladies who expects every gentleman she speaks to, every gentleman she is introduced to, to suddenly fall at her feet and express such a great desire for her company and her consideration that they can do nothing else but wait in the hope that it will be so." His eyes shot to Tabitha's, who stared back at him in astonishment, surprised by his vehemence. "I do not mean to question your judgment, Lady Croome, but Lady Emma is—"

"You are being quite ridiculous," Lord Jennings interrupted in a tone of voice that brooked no argument. "Lady Croome has picked an excellent young lady to bring to your attention, and your immediate concern is that the lady in question is too aware of her own importance in society?" He snorted and narrowed his eyes, pointing one finger out towards Lord Yarmouth. "If you will make such a quick decision about a lady having barely spoken to her, then I think it is *you* who is rather too filled with your own importance."

Tabitha did not know what to say to this, seeing Lord Yarmouth's reluctance and finding herself both equally frustrated and, for whatever reason, mightily relieved. It was an emotion that she battled furiously, not wishing to hope for anything but good for Lord Yarmouth and yet finding that she struggled to do precisely that.

"I have said I will dance with her," Lord Yarmouth said after a moment, although his expression was now a little ashamed, for his gaze had dropped to the floor and there was color in his face that had not been present beforehand. "That should satisfy you all, should it not?"

"Why did she appear so disappointed?" Tabitha asked before she could stop herself, a little surprised at the sharp glance that he sent her. "You took her dance card, and when you returned it, she did not look as pleased as I might have expected."

Lord Yarmouth rubbed the back of his neck with one hand for a moment or two before answering. "Because," he said slowly, "she had a waltz remaining, and I presume she expected me to take that one."

"I see," Tabitha murmured, looking at Lady Ashbrook and seeing the understanding on her face. Understanding that she herself felt also. "Well, I do not think we shall hold that against you."

A look of relief passed over Lord Yarmouth's face. "No?"

"No, indeed not," Lady Ashbrook replied briskly. "A young lady ought not to seek out a waltz from a gentleman she has only just become acquainted with." Her eyes flickered towards Tabitha for a moment, a question in her gaze that Tabitha could not quite make out. "We shall not blame you for that."

"But we shall state that you ought not to make such

quick judgments on the lady," Lord Jennings stated with a grin. "You will call upon her tomorrow, then?"

Lord Yarmouth opened his mouth to state that he would *not* do so, only to close it again slowly. With a deep and pained sigh, he spread out his hands. "If I do so, will you then permit me to step away from her if I think that there is nothing of interest there?" he asked as Lord Jennings grinned. "There are, I think, many other suggestions that Lady Croome has for me." His eyes darted to hers, a hopeful look therein, and Tabitha nodded in response, ignoring the painful stabbing of her heart. "Will that satisfy you all?"

"Indeed," Tabitha forced herself to say as Lord Jennings muttered something about hoping that Lord Yarmouth would not be this disinclined towards *all* the ladies that he met. "Now, when is your dance?"

Lord Yarmouth stared at her for a moment as though he had quite forgotten what she was talking of, only to whirl around. "It is this next dance!" he exclaimed, clearly horrified that he had almost behaved in a most ungentlemanly like manner. "I must go in search of her."

"I do not think you shall have to look far," Lady Ashbrook replied with a quiet laugh. "She is to your left, Lord Yarmouth, and talking to Lord Smythe in a most animated fashion!"

Tabitha could not help but laugh as Lord Yarmouth muttered something under his breath, stood quietly for a moment to compose himself before making his way directly towards Lady Emma, who had, it seemed, been waiting for him to notice her for her eyes darted to his in a moment, and her smile jumped to her lips.

"You think it entertaining, I think," Lady Ashbrook murmured, taking Tabitha's arm as Lord Jennings began to speak to another gentleman who had come near to them all. "Or is it relief?"

"Relief?" Tabitha repeated, not wanting to permit her friend to know all that was within her heart. "I can assure you, I feel nothing but irritation that Lord Yarmouth would dismiss a lady with such haste. Why, during Hyde Park, he refused to even be introduced to two young ladies that I had considered, and now this evening, he has quite turned away from Lady Emma without even dancing with her or conversing at length." She shook her head and tried to sigh, fully aware that her heart was pleased at this turn of events, even though she could not quite understand why.

Why did she feel such a great reluctance to seek out yet more young ladies for Lord Yarmouth's consideration? Was it because she feared losing the very dear friendship that had grown between them? Their acquaintance would have to change significantly when the time came for Lord Yarmouth to be married.

Nodding to herself and entirely unaware of Lady Ashbrook's searching gaze, Tabitha decided that this must be the reason for her own odd emotions when it came to doing as Lord Yarmouth had asked. She considered Lord Yarmouth to be one of her dearest friends, and the thought of that friendship fragmenting, as it must do when it came time for him to wed, was a painful thought indeed.

"And you cannot imagine why Lord Yarmouth has, so quickly, pushed aside both Lady Emma and the ladies in

Hyde Park?" Lady Ashbrook asked, her voice gentle as she picked up a glass of champagne and handed it to Tabitha before taking one for herself. "There is no understanding within you regarding that?"

Tabitha tilted her head for a moment, then laughed. "I think Lord Yarmouth is still struggling to accept that he must marry," she said as Lady Ashbrook watched her closely. "Therefore, he will find fault with a lady out of fear that, should he truly consider her, he will have no other choice but to begin to court her. That, I think, is his reason for doing so. I must hope, in time, that such an attitude changes, else there shall not be any young ladies left for his consideration!"

Lady Ashbrook did not smile but instead held Tabitha's gaze for a moment before sighing gently and looking away. "Perhaps you are right," she said as Tabitha frowned, wondering why her friend did not join in with her merriment. "But mayhap, in time, another reason will reveal itself."

"Another reason?" Tabitha repeated, all the more confused as to what Lady Ashbrook meant. "What might you consider that to be?"

Lady Ashbrook smiled back at her, her eyes gleaming slightly. "One that Lord Yarmouth is perhaps as yet unaware of," she said cryptically. "Come now; it does not matter. Let us watch the end of the dance and prepare ourselves to hear the many, *many* faults that Lady Emma will have and that Lord Yarmouth cannot bring himself to endure." She laughed, and Tabitha, choosing to set aside whatever it was that Lady Ashbrook had been trying to suggest, smiled back at her friend.

"Very well," she said with a shake of her head. "Although quite what he will have to say after a mere dance, I cannot imagine!"

Another burst of laughter escaped from Lady Ashbrook. "Can you not?" she asked with a broad smile. "Then let us wait with anticipation to hear all that is said of her. I can assure you, there will be very little good!"

Tabitha arched one eyebrow but said nothing, watching Lord Yarmouth and Lady Emma as their dance came to a close. Lady Emma was smiling warmly, but Lord Yarmouth's expression showed no delight or interest at all. Sighing inwardly, Tabitha found a smile coming to her lips as she watched, even though he was throwing aside her suggestion of a particular lady without a good deal of consideration. Just what was it Lady Ashbrook had meant? And why, she asked herself, did Lord Yarmouth's disinterest bring such cheer to her soul when she should, by rights, be feeling the entire opposite? Her brow furrowed as she let these questions sink into her heart. This situation was making things all rather confusing, indeed.

CHAPTER SEVEN

"And my daughter is an excellent musician," Lady Blackmore said as Oliver picked up his teacup and drained the last of it, praying that his time would soon be at an end. "I should very much like it if, one day, you might be able to hear her play."

"That is a kind suggestion, mama," Lady Emma said quickly, her eyes trained on Oliver as he tried to show even a flicker of interest. "But mayhap Lord Yarmouth does not much care for music." Her eyebrow lifted as she shot him a questioning glance. "What are your interests, Lord Yarmouth?"

Forcing himself to behave as properly as would be expected, Oliver gave her a quick smile. "I am fond of music," he said as Lady Blackmore beamed with evident delight. "I do not play anything particularly well, however."

"Then I should be glad to play and sing for you, whenever you might wish it," Lady Emma said quickly before glancing at her mother. "I also read aloud at times and have been told that my voice is very soothing indeed."

Oliver dragged another smile onto his face, thinking to himself that Lady Emma was one of the most self-important creatures he had ever had the chance to meet. "I am sure it is so," he answered, but not before Lady Blackmore had begun to speak of her daughter's many accolades again. Oliver heard of Lady Emma's reading, her singing, her musicianship, her artistry, her education, her love of nature and being out of doors, her fondness for birds that sang in the trees and for the deer that could be seen from her bedchamber at her father's estate. He knew all about the lady's many qualities, but she, he realized, had asked him very little about his own interests or the like. In fact, all the ladies appeared to be doing was pressing upon him just how wonderful Lady Emma was.

The realization did not please him. Lady Emma might be the most astonishing and accomplished young lady in all of London but having an arrogance about her was very displeasing. It was not a quality that Oliver admired or wished for in a lady, and certainly, his requirement for a wife did not mean that he had to accept such a thing from Lady Emma. Lady Croome had other ladies that she thought suitable for him, and Oliver had no intention of considering Lady Emma any longer. She was quite displeasing, he thought, desperately waiting for a break in the conversation between mother and daughter so that he might take his leave.

Thankfully, a scratch at the door broke through their eagerness to tell him all of Lady Emma's accomplishments and, when another gentleman was announced, Oliver rose to his feet with great relief.

"Thank you for allowing me to join you this afternoon," he said, bowing low but making certain not to state that he would wish for any further acquaintance with the lady. "Good afternoon, Lady Blackmore. Good afternoon, Lady Emma."

Lady Emma had dropped into a beautiful curtsy, her eyes demure as she allowed herself to lift her gaze to his, blinking slowly under long black eyelashes.

Oliver was unmoved.

"Good afternoon, Lord Yarmouth," Lady Blackmore said as Lady Emma murmured the same. "You are welcome to call upon my daughter whenever you might wish. You shall always be welcome."

"I thank you," Oliver replied but did not state that he should like very much to call upon the lady again. Instead, he turned and, with a quick murmur to the gentleman who had entered, made his way to the door and stepped through it without even glancing back behind him.

His chest lifted as he drew in a long breath, glad beyond expression that his meeting with Lady Emma was at an end. Try as he might, he could not find anything about the lady that he thought to be at all of interest. She was beautiful, yes, but there were many things lacking in her character that he could not simply ignore. Beauty would fade, and he did not want to marry a lady who had so many irritating qualities and who would, most likely, expect him to dote upon her merely because of who she was and how accomplished she believed herself to be.

No, pride and arrogance were not qualities he could accept from a lady, and thus, it was with both relief and contentment that he made his way from the house.

Pausing for a moment, Oliver considered what he was to do next. Part of him wanted to go directly to Lady Croome, to inform her that he was now quite certain that Lady Emma would *not* do and finding himself wondering at what would come into her expression when he told her such a thing. There was a faint hope that she might look relieved, even glad, but that thought was immediately thrown aside. That was a foolish thought and not one that he would entertain. No, most likely, Lady Croome would encourage him to step out with her again at once, so that she might try to find the next young lady she considered for him and, for whatever reason, Oliver was reluctant to do so with such haste.

"Lord Yarmouth?"

He looked to his right and saw Lord and Lady Ashbrook walking towards him and, much to his surprise, Lady Croome coming along with them. They were all looking at him expectantly, and he realized with a jolt that their presence had, in all likelihood, been planned so that they might be nearby when his visit with Lady Emma had come to an end.

"Good afternoon," he said as Lord Ashbrook inclined his head. "Are you also intending to call upon someone here?" He gestured to the street, seeing how Lady Croome grinned and dropped her head forward so that he could not see her expression as easily. "Or is it that you seek only to know just how the meeting between myself and Lady Emma went?"

"The latter," Lady Ashbrook told him firmly. "After all, you did tell Lady Croome the time that you were to take tea with the lady and we could not simply sit about at home and wait for you to inform us as to your decision about the lady!" She glanced to Lady Croome, who did not say a word but stayed precisely where she was, her gaze lowered to the ground. "Although from your expression, might I surmise that all has not gone as well as you might have hoped?"

"I had no particular hope," Oliver replied with as much dignity as he could muster. "Unfortunately, I was proved correct in my thinking that Lady Emma is spoiled and thinks much too highly of herself." He looked at Lady Croome, expecting to see disappointment in her eyes, but much to his astonishment, the corners of her mouth lifted, although she did her utmost to hide it from him. Instead, a look of concern spread through her features, her eyes crinkling gently at the corners, her head tilting just a fraction, but Oliver did not quite believe it to be genuine.

Lady Ashbrook sighed and patted her husband's arm. "How grateful I am that we have found such contentment, Lord Ashbrook," she said as her husband smiled down at her. "It appears to be much more difficult than I remember."

"Then let us be glad that you shall not have to go through such a thing again," Lord Ashbrook replied, lifting his wife's hand and pressing a quick kiss to her palm, which made Lady Ashbrook blush as though she were a debutante being given a compliment by a gentleman she thought very highly of.

Oliver frowned to himself, realizing that there was a part of him that wished very much to have such tenderness in any future relationship he might have, whoever his wife was to be. But how could he gain such a thing when he would barely know the lady he was to marry? Closing his eyes, Oliver shoved the desire away, forcing it to the back of his mind and doing all he could to think of something other than what he had seen before him. It was foolishness to hope for such a thing, for it was not usual for a husband and wife to have such affection between them. No, he would have to be quite practical about the manner and expect nothing more than a companion who would be quite suitable for him and would do all he required as a wife. Affection between husband and wife was rare and, despite his desire to choose a wife of his own, at a time when he felt quite able, he knew now that such decisions had been taken entirely out of his hands.

"Well," Lady Croome said, her voice breaking into his thoughts and forcing him back to the present. "What say we take a short stroll into town in the hope of meeting one of the other young ladies I have considered for you?" She looked at him with a smile on her face, although it did not quite reach her eyes. Was she already weary of her task? Or was she upset that her first choice for him had not gone as well as she had hoped?

"I should be glad to go into town with you, Lady Croome," he said slowly, "but if you would not mind terribly, I should much rather simply enjoy the afternoon instead of being asked to consider someone new." One shoulder lifted in a half shrug. "There is time enough, is there not?"

Lady Croome considered for a moment and then nodded slowly. "There is, certainly," she agreed as Lord and Lady Ashbrook exchanged glances. "I do hope you are not disappointed with my first efforts?"

The urge to reassure her swept through him. "No, not in the least!" he exclaimed, reaching out one hand to settle on her arm for just a moment. "Lady Emma is, as you have said, more than suitable in terms of her standing in society, her father's title, and the dowry that she would bring. In addition," he added, coloring just a little, "she has a great beauty that I could not fail to notice. But it is her lack of beauty within her character that concerns me, that is all."

This seemed to settle Lady Croome's concerns, for her smile grew and her eyes became bright. "Thank you for explaining so to me," she told him as he withdrew his hand. "I confess that I do not know much of Lady Emma, but if you have decided that she is not a suitable match, then I must hope that my second suggestion is a much more preferable one." Seeing how he grimaced, Lady Croome let out a quiet laugh. "But we need not force any introductions this afternoon if you do not wish it. Shall we perhaps go to Gunter's?" She looked up at Lord and Lady Ashbrook, who both nodded eagerly. "It is a fine day, and an ice would be just the thing."

"I quite agree," Oliver stated, offering his arm to Lady Croome, who took it at once. "And thank you for your understanding, Tabitha," he continued in a quieter voice.

"You know that I do greatly appreciate your judgment and your consideration in these matters."

"Yes, I know." She dimpled up at him, and Oliver found himself smiling back, a sense of well-being washing over him. "I am sure we will have a very enjoyable afternoon."

"Indeed, we will," he breathed, enjoying the company, the warmth of the sun, and the sense of freedom that had returned to him, albeit for only a short time. He would soon have to prepare to meet the second lady of Lady Croome's choosing, but, for the moment, he resolved to put such thoughts aside and to focus solely on his company at present. That, he knew, would bring him more happiness than anything else, and the more he considered Lady Croome, the more grateful he became for her wise words, her company, and her kindness. She really was a truly extraordinary creature, and Oliver felt blessed to know her as his friend.

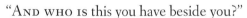

"AND WHO IS this you have beside you?"

Oliver flinched as Lady Croome sent an apologetic smile in his direction. The introduction to one Miss Frederica Bartlett was not going particularly well, even though he could hardly blame the lady herself for that.

"Give me leave to present the Earl of Yarmouth, Lady Stanway," Lady Croome replied as Miss Bartlett's mother took a step forward and, in doing so, made her daughter stumble to the right. Quickly, Oliver grasped her hand so that she would not fall and bring about a great deal of shame to herself, making the young lady blush furiously, her eyes fixed to the floor as she murmured a thank you.

Lady Stanway did not even appear to notice, such was her interest in Oliver himself.

"The Earl of Yarmouth, you say?" she breathed, glancing at Lady Croome. "Capital! Capital indeed!" She curtsied, and Miss Bartlett did the same, her face still a shining crimson. "How excellent to make your acquaintance, Lord Yarmouth. This is my daughter, Miss Frederica Bartlett, as Lady Croome has just informed you. I am sure she would be very glad of a dance or two from you!"

This was forward of Lady Stanway, and astonishment rippled over Oliver, rendering him speechless for a moment or two. Miss Bartlett looked at her mother askance, then closed her eyes and dropped her head in embarrassment.

Oliver felt his heart twist with sympathy—an emotion he had not expected to feel. Miss Bartlett was being prevented from saying a single word to him by her own overbearing mother, and that, in itself, was something that Oliver could identify with. He knew very well what it was like to have a parent who was solely determined to push and prod until a certain matter of course was taken, and, given that he felt such a sympathy, he did not immediately turn away from the lady.

"Miss Bartlett," he said, bowing again. "It would please me greatly to dance with you."

Miss Bartlett's eyes rounded in surprise, and it took her a moment or two to slip the dance card from her wrist and hand it to him. Evidently, she had fully expected him to decline, given the rudeness of her mother, but Oliver found himself quite willing to take the opportunity to speak to Miss Bartlett alone, albeit during the dance.

"The country dance would suit me very well," he said, looking up at Miss Bartlett, who immediately nodded, her face still red with mortification. "And perhaps the cotillion?"

Miss Bartlett blinked rapidly in evident astonishment that she would not only be given one dance, but two, only to nod feverishly whilst her mother began to throw various compliments in Oliver's direction as though he were doing something quite magnanimous in offering her daughter such attentions.

"Until the country dance then, Miss Bartlett," Oliver said loudly, bowing quickly so that he might take his leave. Turning away from the lady and her obnoxious mother, he let out a long breath of relief whilst Lady Croome watched him speculatively.

"Lady Stanway is overbearing, is she not?" he asked as Lady Croome's lips twisted. "Little wonder her daughter has so few dances filled this evening!"

"I think it a sorry affair," Lady Croome replied, her voice filled with compassion. "I have spoken to Miss Bartlett on various occasions, but it is difficult to have a conversation with her without her mother joining us to give *her* opinion or, in fact, to steer the subject to one that she wishes to discuss." A heavy sigh left her, and she looked up at him, appearing a little troubled. "I believe Miss Bartlett to be a very delicate creature," she continued quietly. "Someone who has a very sweet nature indeed and who will always be contented and thankful. She has no arrogance of her own but rather needs to be given opportunity to speak as she wishes."

"I understand," Oliver replied, aware that whilst Miss Bartlett was lovely in her features, he found her quietness rather difficult. "You think that I need to have time with her alone so that I might be able to speak to the lady and discover the truth about her character."

Lady Croome nodded, her smile now returning. "That is it precisely," she said as he nodded slowly. "You treated her very well, offering her two dances. That is not something that has happened to her very often, I am sure."

"Which reminds me," Oliver replied with a grin. "You and I have not yet chosen a dance together, Tabitha." Holding up one hand to silence the protest that he knew would be coming from her lips, he chuckled. "There is no good reason for us not to do so simply because I am seeking to court another," he said, aware of the light fading from her eyes and how her smile dimmed just a little. "There is no need to concern yourself, truly. No one will think any worse of me for stepping out with you if that is what you are worried about. I am sure they will not even notice it!"

"Then what dance is it you wish to take?" Lady Croome replied, pulling out her dance card and handing it to him. "The quadrille?"

"The waltz," he said firmly. Taking the card from her, he wrote his name quickly and then handed it back to her, a little surprised at the glow of warmth that appeared in her eyes.

"The waltz?" she repeated, taking the card back from him and looking down at it. "I thank you."

He shrugged. "It makes certain that I cannot be asked to dance it with any other young lady that might seek out my acquaintance tonight," he told her honestly. "You are to protect me this evening, Lady Croome!"

She did not smile up at him as he had expected, and his laugh faded away to nothing, leaving him wondering if he had upset her in some way. They looked at each other for a long moment, with Lady Croome's expression so veiled that he could not even guess as to what she might be feeling.

"Lord Yarmouth!"

His attention was pulled away as someone hailed him. It was an old acquaintance who had, it seemed, returned to London. Grinning broadly, Oliver turned back to tell Lady Croome that he would speak to her again very soon, only to realize that she was gone.

Something stabbed hard at his heart, and he unconsciously pressed his hand to his chest, his eyes searching for her, but there was no sign. She had evidently faded quickly into the crowd, stepping away from him when his attention had been pulled elsewhere, and something about her expression still troubled him.

"Lord Yarmouth!"

Frustrated, Oliver turned around and made his way towards his friend, trying to set aside his irritation and his concern for Lady Croome. Whatever it was, he would speak to her of it later in the hope that she would tell him what it was that troubled her. He only prayed that he had done nothing to upset her, not when she was doing so very much for him.

"How good to see you this evening!" his acquaintance began, and Oliver found himself drawn into the conversation almost at once, but no matter how long they spoke, no matter how much they laughed and reminisced, at the back of his mind remained Lady Croome and that strange expression that had lingered on her face.

CHAPTER EIGHT

Tabitha tried her utmost to be glad that Miss Bartlett had been permitted to join both herself and Lord Yarmouth for an afternoon walk, but try as she might, she could not seem to summon any enthusiasm whatsoever. Standing aside, she watched as Lord Yarmouth extended a hand to Miss Bartlett to help her into the carriage and forced a smile to her lips, seeing how Lord Yarmouth nodded encouragingly to the young lady who appeared anxious to be stepping out away from her mother.

"And you are quite certain, Lady Croome, that you have no particular interest in Lord Yarmouth yourself?"

Tabitha startled violently as the voice of Lady Stanway reached her ears. Heat wound its way through her chest and up into her face as she realized that the lady had, in fact, shouted her question in Tabitha's direction rather than coming over to speak to her privately.

"We are very great friends," she replied, hating that

her face had turned scarlet. "I will, of course, make sure that your daughter is well looked after."

Lady Stanway waved a hand as if to say that there was no particular requirement for Tabitha to do so before turning around and making her way back into the house.

"A very peculiar lady indeed," Lord Yarmouth murmured out of the corner of his mouth, offering her his hand as she made to climb into the carriage. "You are not too embarrassed, I hope?"

The worry in his eyes made her smile, and she squeezed his fingers lightly. "I am quite all right," she said, thinking that he clearly was already aware of how she was feeling—although whether that came from the color of her face or from the friendship between them, she was not certain. "Shall we go?"

Lord Yarmouth nodded, and Tabitha climbed up into the carriage, coming to sit next to Miss Bartlett, who was, by now, the color of scarlet. Clearly, she had heard her mother screeching from the front of the townhouse.

"A wonderful day," Tabitha said warmly, hoping to encourage the young lady. "St James' Park will be quite lovely this afternoon."

"Indeed it will," Lord Yarmouth agreed, sitting down and rapping lightly on the roof. "Although you must say if you feel fatigued, Miss Bartlett. The sun can be very hot, you know."

Miss Bartlett nodded but did not say anything in response. Instead, she simply turned her head and looked out the window, leaving Tabitha and Lord Yarmouth with equal expressions of helplessness. The journey to St James' Park was awkward, with stilted conversation and without even a single smile from Miss Bartlett herself. Tabitha felt herself grow embarrassed at the lady's demeanor, for whilst she had been acquainted with Miss Bartlett before, she had always managed to have a fairly enjoyable conversation with her, until, inevitably, her mother reappeared. It now appeared, however, that Miss Bartlett intended to remain almost entirely silent in the company of Lord Yarmouth, which was not at all what Tabitha had expected. Would Lord Yarmouth think that she had *deliberately* chosen someone such as Miss Bartlett? She prayed that he would not think worse of her for it!

Thankfully, the carriage soon came to a stop at St James' Park, and, within a few minutes, the three of them were beginning to walk along one of the paths, which were fairly busy given the time of day. Miss Bartlett said nothing of importance, but there was a small smile on her face as she walked along, which Tabitha was very relieved to see.

"Do you enjoy being in London, Miss Bartlett?" Lord Yarmouth asked, and the smile on Miss Bartlett's face disappeared in an instant. In fact, she appeared to be almost anxious, for her fingers twisted together and a paleness crept into her cheeks.

"Y—yes, my lord," she stammered, looking to Tabitha for evident reassurance. "And you?"

Lord Yarmouth looked pleased that she had asked him such a thing. "Indeed, I have found it very enjoyable thus far," he said, although Tabitha hid a smile when he shot her a hard glance, silently reminding her not to mention any of his difficulties at present. "It is always good to make new acquaintances. Tell me, Miss Bartlett, have you any friends here in London that you are glad to see again?"

Tabitha, a smile still lingering on her face, looked back at Miss Bartlett, entirely astonished to see a small tremor running through the lady's thin frame as she came to a dead stop, looking up at Lord Yarmouth with terrified eyes.

"What has my mother told you?" she breathed as Lord Yarmouth began to frown, his brows furrowing and his eyes darkening just a little. "Has she said something that I should know?"

"Nothing of any importance," Tabitha said quickly, looking at Lord Yarmouth, who, seeing her sharp gaze, quickly began to deny such a thing also.

"I can assure you, Miss Bartlett, that your mother has not spoken to me about anything to do with you," he said as Miss Bartlett pressed her fingers to her mouth, her skin milk-white and her eyes rounded with evident fright. "Pray, do not trouble yourself in such a way!"

It took a few minutes for Miss Bartlett to calm herself. Slowly, her hands separated, and her arms fell to her sides. Her head lowered, and her lips trembled. Not quite certain whether or not to simply disregard what had occurred or if she ought to step forward and comfort the lady in some way, Tabitha shot a despairing look towards Lord Yarmouth, who gave her a small shrug of his shoulders. Clearly, he was just as lost as she.

"I—I am sure Lord Yarmouth has a great deal he wishes to speak to you about, Miss Bartlett," Tabitha found herself saying, ignoring the way that Lord

Yarmouth's eyes widened with sudden horror. "Why do you not walk with him for a time? I shall be only a few steps behind." Smiling encouragingly, she gestured for Miss Bartlett to step forward before turning her gaze to Lord Yarmouth, who had not moved either. Widening her eyes and tilting her head furiously in the lady's direction, she let out a breath of relief when he finally cleared his throat and came to stand alongside Miss Bartlett, who finally lifted her head and gave him a small smile.

"Tell me about your family, Miss Bartlett," Lord Yarmouth said, beginning to walk again and, much to Tabitha's relief, Miss Bartlett fell into step beside him. "Or about your father's estate, if you please. I confess I know very little of it all."

Tabitha walked a few steps behind them both, thinking hard about what had just occurred. Miss Bartlett had gone quite to pieces in front of them both and without any clear reason as to why. There was a fear of her mother, that was for certain, but quite what that anxiety was about in particular, Tabitha did not know. Was it something she ought to ask Miss Bartlett about? Or was this a matter that Lord Yarmouth would discover in time, should things go well?

Should things go well.

The final few words of her thoughts repeated themselves over and over in her mind, making Tabitha feel almost sick with anxiety that she could not quite explain. It was as though any thought of Lord Yarmouth's future made her both upset and deeply uneasy. Her initial thought that she wanted his company, his friendship, to remain exactly as it was at present was, she considered, the most reasonable explanation, but it was foolish. Lady Ashbrook had been her acquaintance before she had been married, and now, as a married lady, she was just as dear to Tabitha as ever. Why should it be different with Lord Yarmouth? Yes, she might not have as close an acquaintance as before, but that was entirely to be expected.

"I shall simply have to become close to *Lady* Yarmouth, whoever she may be," she said quietly to herself, trying her best not to give in to the pang of sorrow that struck her heart at those words. Try as she might, she could not seem to rid herself of such a feeling, and even her attempts to remain quite practical did not appear to be doing anything to help.

"What say you, Lady Croome?"

Tabitha lifted her head and gave her attention to Lord Yarmouth and Miss Bartlett again, who had both stopped to look at her. Miss Bartlett, Tabitha noted, appeared to be much more at ease now, no longer looking as tense or anxious, although she was not smiling.

"I am afraid I was quite lost in thought, Lord Yarmouth," she said pleasantly, praying that he would not ask her what she had been thinking of. "Did you have something you wished to speak to me about?"

Lord Yarmouth smiled at her. "It was merely to question whether or not you think Lord and Lady Melville's masquerade ball will be just as exceptional as last year," he said as Tabitha laughed. "You attended it last Season if I recall correctly?"

"I did," Tabitha agreed with a bright smile. "And it was quite magnificent. I am very much looking forward to attending this year also." She smiled at Miss Bartlett. "Will you be going, Miss Bartlett?"

"I—I hope so," Miss Bartlett replied. "My mother has not yet informed me as to whether or not she has accepted, although I am quite certain she would have done so if it is an exceptional occasion."

"I am glad to hear it," Lord Yarmouth said as Tabitha found it difficult to keep her smile fixed in place. "You must make certain to come and find me amongst the crowd, Miss Bartlett. I shall not be very difficult to spot, even with a mask!"

Miss Bartlett blushed, and Tabitha looked away; even the memory of Lord Yarmouth and his poor attempt at a mask from last year's ball did not bring even a ghost of a smile to her lips.

"Shall we perhaps return to the carriage?" Lord Yarmouth asked, offering Miss Bartlett his arm. "We do not want to be too long away from your mother."

Tabitha watched as Miss Bartlett looked from Lord Yarmouth to his proffered arm and then to Tabitha. She expected the girl to step forward and accept it within a few moments but was left entirely astonished as she gave a small shake of her head and then made her way to join Tabitha without accepting Lord Yarmouth's offer. Blinking in astonishment but doing her utmost not to reveal it, she merely smiled back at Lord Yarmouth, whose eyes had rounded in surprise, before making her way slowly back towards the carriage with Miss Bartlett beside her.

Miss Bartlett, it seemed, was a very curious young lady indeed.

~

"And do you mean to say that she did not accept him?"

"It was most extraordinary," Tabitha agreed, shaking her head as Lady Ashbrook's eyes widened. "I would have thought that Miss Bartlett, having accepted a walk in the park from Lord Yarmouth, would have been glad to have taken his arm. After all, Lord Yarmouth is an earl and she the daughter of a viscount—surely she would want to *encourage* his intentions!"

Lady Ashbrook nodded, the peacock feathers on the side of her mask sweeping back and forth. "And did you have an opportunity to speak to Lord Yarmouth thereafter?"

"I did," Tabitha replied, a trifle hesitantly. "He did not appear to be at all upset about her refusal, although there was a sense of astonishment at her behavior." She glanced at Lady Ashbrook, who was watching her with careful eyes, hidden slightly behind her mask. "He stated that he found Miss Bartlett to be very reserved indeed, which was not something I had expected. However, she had begun to speak a little more openly to him during the short time that they walked together, which made her refusal to accept his arm all the more astonishing."

"I do not understand it," Lady Ashbrook agreed with a shake of her head. "I would have thought that she would have been eager to make the most of her conversation with him. Did anything else occur that made you believe she was not as eager as she might have appeared?"

Instantly, the strange reaction that Miss Bartlett had exhibited in mention of her mother came back to

Tabitha's mind, and she quickly related it to her friend, who looked all the more astonished.

"I did not mention it thereafter," Tabitha finished with a shrug of her shoulders. "I did not know what to say and even whether or not I should speak of it again. I do hope that, in time—and should all go well with Lord Yarmouth and Miss Bartlett—that she will speak to him of her troubles."

Lady Ashbrook let out her breath slowly, her lips pulled thin. "I should suggest, Tabitha, that Miss Bartlett seems a complicated young lady. Her mother is *quite* overbearing and has clearly had something of an effect on Miss Bartlett's character. I would be surprised if Lord Yarmouth was as willing to continue with her."

"He has something of a compassionate heart, however," Tabitha argued quietly. "Initially, he was a little deterred from her, but he was not willing to give up as he had done before." She did not mention that she had been required to almost force the continuation of their acquaintance but instead, continued to defend him. "We may find that he is sympathetic enough to her situation that he is willing to continue with the acquaintance regardless."

Lady Ashbrook sighed but said nothing, walking together with Tabitha towards the open French doors where they might gain a little fresh air.

"I do not know," Tabitha murmured, half to herself. "It is all very difficult. I did not think Miss Bartlett would be as silent nor as unwilling as she appeared."

"You are doing your very best, I am sure," Lady

Ashbrook replied, pressing Tabitha's hand. "Goodness, this is quite lovely, do you not think?"

Her mind momentarily pulled from her troubled thoughts, Tabitha looked all about her and immediately agreed with the sentiment. The garden was lit with lanterns, and there were many beautiful decorations hung from the shrubs and bushes. Lord and Lady Melville had done magnificently, and Tabitha smiled in contentment. This night was very beautiful, indeed.

A sudden whispering caught Tabitha's attention, and she stopped dead, catching Lady Ashbrook's arm.

"What is—?"

Tabitha shook her head, motioning her friend to be silent. Lady Ashbrook did as she was asked without question, frowning hard as she looked at Tabitha, but Tabitha was much too distracted with hearing the sound of someone crying. Evidently, Lady Ashbrook heard it also, for within a few moments, her eyes widened, and she stared hard at Tabitha, clearly uncertain as to what they were to do.

"Wait," Tabitha mouthed, looking around the gardens and realizing that there were very few guests out of doors. It would soon be time for the masks to be removed and for the invited guests to reveal their true identity to each other, and no one wanted to miss such a thing. Turning her head, she listened hard again, hearing the crying become a little louder.

"What should we do?" Lady Ashbrook asked, but Tabitha had already left their path and was making her way towards the sound. There could be many reasons why someone was upset certainly, but to be crying at a masquerade ball, out in the gardens could mean, to Tabitha's mind, that there was someone in distress. Someone, perhaps, who had allowed a rake to capture their attentions for long enough to pull them into the gardens, only to realize precisely what they wanted.

"Who is there?" she asked as the sound of crying quickly abated. "I can hear you still, and my friend, Lady Ashbrook, is standing by the path." She kept her tone measured, not wanting to express any sort of threat to whoever was hidden in the shadows. "I want only to make certain that you are not unwell nor broken-hearted. In addition, should you require a discreet chaperone to return you to the ballroom, I would be glad to do so."

"Lady—Lady Croome?"

The tearful voice was familiar to Tabitha's ears, but she could not immediately place it. Frowning, she cleared her throat. "Yes, it is Lady Tabitha Croome," she said in a somewhat formal manner. "Are we acquainted?"

The sniffing began again in earnest, and, much to Tabitha's dismay, the sound of a male voice caught her ears. Whoever was speaking to the lady, it appeared that she was not alone.

"Pray, do not think ill of me, Lady Croome," said the voice in between heavy sniffing. "There is more to this situation than it first appears, and you know very well that my mother will *never* consent to such a thing."

The remark about the lady's mother immediately made everything fall into place.

"Miss Bartlett?" Tabitha breathed, her heart pounding with a sudden astonishment. "Is it you who speaks to me?"

There was silence for a moment or two, and then the acknowledgment that Tabitha was correct was spoken.

"And who is with you?" Tabitha demanded, praying desperately that it was not Lord Yarmouth. "If they have done you any harm, I shall—"

"No, he has not," Miss Bartlett cried, coming a few steps closer to Tabitha and finally revealing herself to her, although her features were still shrouded in shadow. "Lord Naseby and I intended to elope this evening, but all is undone!" She began to sob as Tabitha stared at the lady with wide eyes, her heart pounding furiously as she tried to take in what was being said.

"Elope?" came a voice from behind her. "You mean to say that you intend to elope with this gentleman, Miss Bartlett? What can you be thinking?"

"My friend, Lady Ashbrook," Tabitha explained, quickly, hearing Miss Bartlett's swift intake of breath. "What she means to say is—"

"I care very deeply for Miss Bartlett," came a low voice as the as yet unintroduced Lord Naseby stepped forward, coming close to the young lady. "I have cared for her for a long time. I have begged Lord Blackmore to permit me to court Miss Bartlett, but he has refused."

Tabitha brows dug low. "And why has he refused?" she asked, afraid that there was something untoward about the fellow.

"Because I am but a viscount and Lord Blackmore wishes his daughter to marry above her station," Lord Naseby replied, his tone one of anger as Miss Bartlett began to cry again. "This was to be our only opportunity to escape, but, alas, it seems as though we are to be parted for good."

Trying to take in all that had been revealed to her, Tabitha understood why Miss Bartlett had behaved as she had done the previous afternoon. She had been afraid that either Tabitha herself or Lord Yarmouth had heard of her acquaintance with Lord Naseby, or that her mother had mentioned the name to Lord Yarmouth instead. It appeared as though the lady did, in fact, care for Lord Naseby very deeply, which was, again, the reason that she had refused Lord Yarmouth's arm. She did not want to betray the gentleman she cared for.

"I see," Tabitha said slowly. "And what has occurred to prevent it, Lord Naseby?"

He sighed, and Miss Bartlett dropped her head on his shoulder. "My carriage wheel was broken this afternoon," he said heavily. "I had to take a hackney to attend this evening, and I cannot simply demand that a hackney drive us to Scotland. They would never manage the same speed as the carriage, meaning that Lord Blackmore would be quite likely to discover us."

"And the only reason I have been able to escape from my mother is because of this masquerade," Miss Bartlett explained, brokenly. "I shall not have such an opportunity again."

Tabitha let out a long breath, looking at Lady Ashbrook, who, for whatever reason, remained silent. There was a choice now before her. Either she could simply wish the couple well and privately tell Lord Yarmouth what she had learned, or she could do something to help them.

The second option was not something that she considered lightly. To do so would be to encourage them to do something that both Lord and Lady Blackmore had expressly forbidden. But neither could she allow herself simply to step away, to see Miss Bartlett so sorrowful and heartbroken that her one opportunity for happiness had been stolen from her.

"You—you may take my carriage," she found herself saying, aware of her friend's gasp of astonishment as well as the stunned silence that followed her words. "I will go with you and instruct my driver as to what he must do."

Lord Naseby was the first to speak, his voice breaking with the great swell of emotion that had obviously grasped him. "Are you quite certain, Lady Croome?" he asked as Miss Bartlett began to cry with earnest. "It is a great burden upon you, surely, for to be without a carriage..."

"It would be a greater burden upon my heart, I can assure you, if I did nothing," Tabitha replied fervently. "Come, we must go before the unmasking is upon us."

A gentle hand tugged Tabitha's sleeve.

"Are you quite certain?" Tabitha turned to Lady Ashbrook in the darkness. "That is quite a decision."

"I am determined," Tabitha replied honestly. "I must do all that I can to help Miss Bartlett, for this sort of affection does not come upon everyone, and, when it does, it must be cherished."

"I am very grateful to you for your understanding," Miss Bartlett whispered, her voice barely loud enough for Tabitha to hear. "Especially after so short an acquaintance."

Tabitha let out a breath, feeling all the more confident in her decision. "It is the right thing to do," she said determinedly. "Come now; we must hurry." And, saying so, she quickly hurried back towards the path, and then, with the others falling in behind her, made her way back into the ballroom.

CHAPTER NINE

"I did not see Miss Bartlett all last evening," Oliver mused, picking up a brandy glass and swirling it around gently. "I confess I find her a most unusual young lady."

Lord Jennings chuckled. "One that you will continue to consider?"

Oliver hesitated. "I—I could not say," he replied slowly. "It is not to say that I do not find her to be of interest to me, and certainly, she has a gentle beauty about her, but that I find the time I spend with her to be..." Tilting his head, he looked at his friend steadily, trying to find the right words. "It can be a little exhausting."

Lord Jennings did not laugh or throw back a teasing remark as Oliver had expected. Instead, he simply nodded musingly and then shrugged. "That might change, with time. It is only the beginning of your acquaintance, is it not?"

"It is," Oliver agreed, "but given that Lady Blackmore

will be a part of my life should I continue with Miss Bartlett, I find that the idea of continuing my acquaintance with the lady to be a difficult one."

Shrugging his shoulders, he frowned hard, trying to reconcile all that he felt and all that he considered. Whilst everything that he said was quite true, there was still something more about his acquaintance with Miss Bartlett that was lacking. Whilst he had been grateful for Lady Croome and her support in encouraging the acquaintance, he had found it very difficult to have even the smallest conversation with Miss Bartlett, despite his attempts. She had begun to relax just a little after a good few minutes, but their discussion had been stilted, and even he had struggled to think of what to say. As they had walked in the park, Oliver had found himself wishing for the ease of manner that came whenever he spoke with Lady Croome. With her, he never once struggled with what to say, with what to remark or comment upon. There had never been any difficulty between them in that regard, not even from their very first conversation! When Lady Croome and Miss Bartlett had walked back to the carriage, leaving him to walk behind, he had found himself unconsciously comparing the two ladies and finding that, no matter what he considered, Lady Croome was always superior.

"I am being foolish, of course," he said aloud, a little irritated with himself. It would not do to compare the two women, especially since he had been acquainted with Lady Croome for some time and had developed an intimacy within their friendship that could not be easily replicated. "I am sure that I should give a little more consideration to Miss Bartlett, especially given that Lady Croome has put so much effort into encouraging the acquaintance." Even as he spoke, Oliver became aware of a small stab of pain entering his heart. Confused, he frowned hard, wondering at why he had felt such a thing simply because he had mentioned Lady Croome and her attempts to find him a suitable bride. He had asked her to do so, had he not? Why then would he feel such a strange emotion when she was being very successful indeed in all that he had asked her?

"Is something troubling you?"

Jerking himself out of his own thoughts, Oliver shook his head quickly. "Nothing," he lied. "Save for what I am to do about Miss Bartlett."

This did not appear to convince Lord Jennings, for his brow lifted, and he looked back at Oliver with a doubtful expression.

"I am conflicted as to whether or not I continue the acquaintance, or if I do nothing but give up and ask Lady Croome for her next suggested lady," Oliver continued hastily, doing his utmost to cover up his own feelings so that he would not have to either continue to consider them himself or speak of them to Lord Jennings. "Miss Bartlett may, in time, begin to speak openly to me, but that will take many weeks, if not months, to achieve, and I should like to, at the very least, *know* the lady fairly well before I wed her."

For some inexplicable reason, this statement brought Lord Jennings to laughter, which only made Oliver all the more confused. Looking back at his friend, he waited until the man's laughter had subsided before spreading his hands in silent question—but Lord Jennings did not answer him as he wished.

"It is of little importance," Lord Jennings said, his lips still pulled into a wide grin. "And I am afraid I cannot advise you regarding Miss Bartlett. That is entirely your own decision, Yarmouth." His smile faded, and an expression of seriousness flooded his features. "Although I would say that anything that requires a great deal of effort must be worth that effort. If you are to continue with Miss Bartlett, then you must expect to consider her seriously as your bride, for you shall put in a great deal of time and energy into discovering her character given that she is both quiet and reluctant to converse with you."

Oliver rubbed one hand over his eyes. "That is quite so," he agreed, grateful for his friend's advice. "Now, perhaps we should consider departing so that my mind is not taken up solely by Miss Bartlett." He smiled at his friend. "If you are quite ready, that is?"

They were both to attend an evening assembly but had not been in any hurry to make their way there. Lord Wimple's evening assembly would be very much like the gentleman himself, they had concluded. Slow to begin, only to burst into life after some hours had passed. However, although Oliver had been initially very glad to wait at home for a few additional hours, he now found himself eager to make his way there at once, if only so that his mind might stop whirring.

It was not that he only considered Miss Bartlett through all of this, but rather that Lady Croome was present in his thoughts also, although he could not quite understand why. There was no reason for him to continue considering her, no real explanation as to why he struggled to remove her from his thinking, but try as he might, she continued to linger there. When he thought of Miss Bartlett, he thought of Lady Croome, comparing the two as though they were in competition. Perhaps, he told himself, it was simply because the intimacy he shared with Lady Croome at present was what he sought from his potential bride to be and, in finding that ease of conversation and manner lacking, he then felt inclined towards Lady Croome herself rather than Miss Bartlett.

"You ask me if we are to make our way to the evening assembly and then continue to sit there as though stupefied!"

Oliver jerked in his seat, looking up to see Lord Jennings giving him a bemused glance.

"My apologies," he said quickly. "I was lost in thought."

"Considering Miss Bartlett again?"

Oliver nodded, ignoring the guilt that flooded him as he lied to his friend. "Yes, yes, of course."

Lord Jennings chuckled and moved towards the door, leaving Oliver to scramble after him. As they walked to the front of the house together, Oliver was left with the uncomfortable feeling that his friend did not quite believe him when it came to expressing what he had been thinking about. There was a knowing gleam in Lord Jennings' eye, but still, Oliver did not want to be honest about his strange thoughts regarding Lady Croome. They would fade away quickly, he told himself. It was only because he was in this situation of being forced to find a bride that he was now struggling with his own considerations. There was nothing more than that.

≈

"GOOD EVENING, LADY CROOME."

Oliver's heart leaped in his chest as Lady Croome dropped into a quick curtsy.

I am merely glad to see her, he told himself as she smiled up at him. *At least with Lady Croome, I am not expected to play the part of a gentleman interested in pursuing a further acquaintance! I can just be as I am at present.*

"You look a little tired, Lord Yarmouth," Lady Croome said with a note of concern in her voice. "Are you quite well?"

"I believe he has a lot on his mind regarding Miss Bartlett," Lord Jennings interrupted before Oliver could say anything. "Very uncertain about the lady, I must say."

Shooting a hard look at Lord Jennings—a look which was not easily accepted for Lord Jennings only grinned and shrugged—Oliver turned his attention back to Lady Croome, seeing her enquiring expression, although the concern had not quite left her eyes.

"I am quite all right," he said as she smiled at him. "Lord Jennings and I have been discussing the merits of Miss Bartlett, that is all."

Lady Croome dropped her gaze, a slight redness flooding her cheeks. Confused, Oliver came a little closer to her, instantly forgetting about Lord Jennings' presence.

"Is something wrong, Tabitha?" he asked quietly, his

words almost drowned out by the sound of the musicians beginning to play. "Has Miss Bartlett said something that I should know of?"

Oliver's chest became a little tight as Lady Croome slowly lifted her head, her eyes searching his face and her tongue licking her lips in a most nervous fashion. His hand found hers in an instant, wanting to know what it was that troubled her and, at the same time, wishing eagerly to take away the anxiety that was clearly written there.

"You must forgive me, Yarmouth," Lady Croome said, her hand pressing his, and it was not until that moment that he realized just how cold her fingers were. "But something has occurred that—"

"Lady Croome!"

In an instant, Lady Croome dropped his hand and turned herself quickly to greet an older lady who had clearly made her way across the room to greet her.

"Good evening, Lady Sutherland," she said quickly, throwing Oliver a glance over her shoulder. "How are you this evening?"

"Very well indeed," Lady Sutherland replied, a light Scottish lilt dancing through her words. Her eyes, Oliver noticed, turned towards him with an eagerness that sent a small chill running down his back, although, of course, he stepped forward and made to greet the lady at once.

"You are acquainted with Lady Sutherland, Lord Yarmouth?" Lady Croome asked, her eyes a little round as she looked up at him. "I believe you met a few Seasons ago."

Oliver nodded, recalling the imposing figure of the

lady he had once been introduced to but whom he had never again spoken to. "It was two years ago, I believe?" he asked, bowing low. "Although I might be mistaken."

Lady Sutherland laughed, her bright manner encouraging Oliver a little.

"You are quite correct, Lord Yarmouth," she said, clearly delighted that he had recalled her. "But I do not think you were ever introduced to my daughter." Her eyes fixed to his, and Oliver, despite his surprise at such a statement, forced himself to remain entirely composed.

"No, I did not," he said with something of a tight smile. "I do not think I ever had the pleasure, Lady Sutherland."

She laughed again, but this time, the sound began to grate on Oliver's ears. A quick glance towards Lady Croome told him that she was a little embarrassed, for there was more color in her cheeks than had been there at the first and her eyes were darting from Lady Sutherland to his face and then back again.

"Then," Lady Sutherland replied, already beginning to turn away, "I shall have the introductions made at once. Do excuse me for a moment, Lord Yarmouth."

The moment Lady Sutherland stepped away, Oliver turned to Lady Croome.

"What is this?" he whispered, his brows lowering. "Another young lady I am to be introduced to?"

He expected Lady Croome to drop her head with embarrassment, to murmur something that he might be able to consider later, but instead, she lifted her chin and looked directly into his face, her red cheeks already beginning to fade.

"I did not think that Lady Sutherland would be as eager to introduce her daughter to you as all that," she said firmly, "but yes, you are quite right. It is another young lady for you to consider—and one that Lady Sutherland herself suggested when she approached me some days ago." One shoulder lifted. "I should be glad of a little appreciation rather than the outright disdain you have shown at present."

Oliver opened his mouth to refute this, only to close it again as he realized that every word Lady Croome had spoken was quite fair. With a heavy sigh, he closed his eyes and tried to calm himself a little. He was not angry with her but perhaps just a little overwhelmed with the swiftness and the confidence of Lady Sutherland's greetings towards him.

"I would have appreciated knowing that Lady Sutherland intended to introduce her daughter, that is all," he said as Lady Croome folded her arms across her chest and glared at him. "It was a surprise."

"And as I have said," Lady Croome replied, frostily, "I did not know that she intended to do so this evening and certainly not with such force. If you recall, we were in the midst of a conversation, and I was about to speak to you of Miss Bartlett but instead was rudely interrupted." Her brows dropped low and she turned her head away. "Forgive me for trying to do what you have asked of me, Yarmouth."

A little ashamed of himself, Oliver began to attempt to apologize, only to see Lady Sutherland coming back towards them with a young lady in tow.

His breath caught.

If this was Lady Sutherland's daughter, then he did not think he had ever seen anyone as beautiful in his life before. She was graceful in her movements, tall and willowy, with a gown of delicate yellow that only drew his attention to her glistening gold curls that, despite being pinned back into a most elegant style, still whispered across her neck and shoulders. Her eyes were a vivid blue and, when she dropped into a curtsy, Oliver was grateful for the few moments he had to bow towards her, for he was struggling to regain his composure, such was his reaction to her beauty.

"Lord Yarmouth, might I present my daughter, Lady Marina," Lady Sutherland said with a broad smile as though she knew precisely what he was thinking and feeling at that present moment. "Marina, this is the Earl of Yarmouth."

"I am very pleased to make your acquaintance."

Lady Marina's voice was gentle, her eyes not searching his face in a bold manner but holding his gaze for just a moment before dropping to the floor. She did not say anything more but instead stood quietly, waiting for his response or for her mother to speak.

"As I am glad to make yours," Oliver found himself saying, his tongue feeling a little too big for his mouth. "Are you quite enjoying the Season thus far?" It was not a question that required a prolonged answer, and her quick response left him struggling to think of what else to say. It was quite ridiculous, of course, for he ought not to base his consideration of a lady on her features alone, but there was something about Lady Marina that seemed to drag him towards her, seemed to force his eyes to linger upon her face.

"My daughter and I were not in London last Season," Lady Sutherland explained quickly. "She was a little unwell but has since recovered."

This did not bring a smile to Lady Marina's face. In fact, there was no reaction at all, for she instead simply continued to keep her eyes fixed to the floor, no smile playing about her lips or frown marring her brow.

"I am glad indeed to hear you have recovered," Oliver found himself saying, quite desperate to have Lady Marina look at him again, eager to discover whether or not he could make her smile. "London society would be all the poorer without your presence, I am sure."

This, finally, brought the lady's eyes back to his for a moment, and, much to his delight, Oliver saw faint color coming to the young lady's cheeks.

"Have you been to the theatre of late?" he asked as Lady Sutherland looked on approvingly. "There was the most magnificent of plays only last week, which I very much enjoyed." He turned to gesture to Lady Croome, who had attended with him. "My dear friend..."

The space where Lady Croome had been standing was now entirely vacant. His words died away, his brow furrowing hard as his eyes tore around the room, searching for her. Why had she disappeared in such a fashion? Was it because of what he had said? He had been irritated with her when he had not had any cause to, but he did not think that such a thing would drive Lady Croome away. Heat climbed up his spine as a flood of guilt covered his heart. He had been much too harsh with her and certainly not at all grateful. That had been wrong of him, and he would need to make amends.

"Lord Yarmouth?"

Dragging his attention back to Lady Sutherland and her daughter, Oliver saw the way that she looked at him speculatively, clearly waiting to hear what else he had to say.

"Forgive me," Oliver replied with a shake of his head. "I thought that Lady Croome still stood here. As I was saying, Lady Marina, I greatly enjoyed the theatre last week, for Lady Croome, Lord Jennings, and I all attended together and had the most excellent of evenings."

Lady Marina's mouth curved gently, and, finally, he saw the lady smile. There was a sense of satisfaction in seeing such a thing, and Oliver felt his heart lift, pushing aside the guilt that had held it in its sway for a time.

"We have an intention to attend the theatre very soon," Lady Sutherland said, once more giving no opportunity for her daughter to speak. "We have not managed to attend as often as I would have liked."

"Then you must permit me to accompany you," Oliver said with a small inclination of his head. "It would be a great honor for me, I assure you."

This seemed to bring about opposite reactions in both the ladies. Lady Marina's eyes widened, and she looked at her mother quickly, although without any sense of eagerness coming from her. Lady Sutherland, on the other hand, was already nodding feverishly, all manner of questions coming to her lips, one after the other. Within a few minutes, an outing to the theatre had been arranged for two days hence, with Oliver promising that he would call for them both in his carriage and would, of course, be glad to show them to his own private box. This seemed to delight Lady Sutherland greatly, for her face was split with a smile, and her eyes danced with excitement.

Lady Marina, on the other hand, had gone a little pale and, whilst she thanked Oliver for his kindness and stated that she was already looking forward to attending with him, there was no happiness in her expression what-soever. Oliver could not quite understand it but chose to ignore the lady's reaction completely. It might very well be that Lady Marina was simply nervous about stepping out with a gentleman. The *ton* would, of course, notice that he had done such a thing and, as such, whispers and rumors would abound, but, Oliver considered, that was to be expected. It was not something that he was at all concerned over, thinking that he would be quite glad to have someone as beautiful as Lady Marina on his arm.

"Ah, they are beginning to dance!" Lady Sutherland cried, turning her head to see some couples starting to form a small group, ready to dance the cotillion. "How wonderful."

The smile on Oliver's face spread all the more quickly. "Should you like to dance, Lady Marina?" he asked, offering her his arm and seeing how she started in evident surprise. "The cotillion is an excellent dance, I think."

Her eyes went to her mother, who gave her an almost imperceptible nod, which Oliver only caught out of the corner of his eye. With a faint appearance of a smile, she took his arm and nodded, allowing him to lead her towards the others. Oliver walked with a sense of pride filling his heart, fully aware that the *beau monde* would notice his companion and would, most likely, marvel at her beauty *and* at the fact that he was the one accompanying her for the dance. His steps felt light, his face captured by a broad smile that he did not think would easily fade.

"An excellent dance indeed," he murmured to himself, stepping apart from Lady Marina and allowing her to find her position.

It was only then that his eyes, straying from Lady Marina for a few moments, found Lady Croome. She was speaking with Lady Ashbrook, and, as he watched, he realized that she was, in fact, upset. There was a sadness in her expression that had not been there before, and Lady Ashbrook settled a comforting hand on her arm, which only made Lady Croome's head bow forward, shaking her head slightly as she did so.

His heart sank as the happiness and pride he had been feeling only a moment before evaporated completely. In seeing Lady Marina, Oliver had completely forgotten Lady Croome. It was as though even the recollection that she was there with him had flown from him in an instant—and that shame bit down hard at him now. How could he have been so unfeeling? To simply forget about his dear friend's company after speaking to her in a harsh manner? It was rude, indeed, and, more than that, clearly injurious to Lady Croome's spirits.

"Lord Yarmouth?"

Dragging his attention back to Lady Marina, he realized that the music had begun, and the couples had started to take their steps. Forced to throw Lady Croome aside yet again, he forced himself to focus entirely on the dance itself, trying his utmost to enjoy the few minutes he had in Lady Marina's company, attempting to regain the happiness that had filled his heart but a minute ago but finding that he could no longer do so. There was still the delight of being in her company, in knowing that the other gentlemen of the *ton* might even be a little envious of him, but it was tainted now. Tainted with the knowledge that he had injured Tabitha, that he had brought her pain, and, in doing so, had shamed himself also.

That is not the way one ought to treat one's friend, he told himself severely. *You must make amends.*

Quite what he was to do, Oliver did not know, but the resolution to do so was already within him. No matter how well this evening went, no matter how enjoyable his time with Lady Marina was, Oliver knew that the only thing he needed to focus on was restoring his relationship with Lady Croome. The rest would come later.

CHAPTER TEN

Tabitha looked at herself in the mirror as her maid finished setting her hair into a simple chignon. Given that she did not expect any afternoon callers and had herself no particular engagements, there was no requirement for her to make any particular effort with her appearance. If she were to be truthful with herself, Tabitha would admit that she did not wish to have company this afternoon either, finding that she almost had to steel herself when it came to considering the dinner party she was to attend this evening.

"Is there anything else I can do for you, my lady?"

Looking at her reflection again and noting the dark smudges under her eyes, Tabitha gave her maid a somewhat wan smile. "No, I thank you," she said as the maid dropped her head, clearly appreciating Tabitha's thanks. "You may lay out my things for this evening, however. I shall be in the drawing-room or library until later."

Rising, Tabitha made her way downstairs, quite looking forward to a quiet afternoon. Lady Ashbrook had insisted that she be permitted to call, but Tabitha had managed to encourage her not to do so, particularly since the dinner party that evening was to be hosted at the Ashbrook's townhouse. Lady Ashbrook would have more than enough to do and certainly did not need to waste her time trying to encourage Tabitha in one way or the other.

"Especially since I am being foolish," Tabitha murmured to herself, walking into the library and picking up the book she had tossed aside on to the table only last evening. She had returned from the evening assembly feeling faint of heart, despite her apparent success with Lady Marina. She had not been able to speak to Lord Yarmouth about Miss Bartlett, but, it seemed, she would have no need to do so. He had been quite taken with Lady Marina, for she had seen the way his eyes had rounded and his mouth had hung a little ajar for just a moment or two as she had approached. And all after he had spoken to her in a very sharp manner, simply because she had been doing what he had asked of her!

Returning home early from the assembly, she had tried her best to retire to bed given the lateness of the hour but had found herself quite unable to do so. Her mind had been filled with none other than Lord Yarmouth. She had seen his face over and over again, recalling how he had stared in astonishment at Lady Marina and finding that, the more she thought of it, the more pain seemed to flood her soul. Despite telling herself that she ought to be glad that there was a clear attraction towards Lady Marina, given that Miss Bartlett was now well on her way to Scotland and certainly would not be returning to London any time soon, there had been a heavy weight on her heart that had not dissipated all through the long hours of the night. She had risen in an attempt to read for a time, so that she would cast her mind away from Lord Yarmouth, only to find herself struggling to read even a single sentence with any sort of concentration or clarity. Frustrated, she had returned to bed but had tossed and turned until finally slipping into an exhausted sleep, just as the sun had begun to rise above the rooftops of London.

She felt no better this morning.

Sighing, Tabitha sat down heavily in a chair, having just rung the bell for tea to be brought to her. Picking up the book, she flipped it open and attempted to begin to read the very next chapter simply so that she might distract herself from her tumbling thoughts.

It took a great deal of effort, but, finally, Tabitha began to find a little solitude in the pages of her novel. It pulled her away from her own life and difficulties into such a story of adventure that she quite forgot all about Lord Yarmouth. Even the tea tray being brought to her did not cause much of a distraction, and thus, Tabitha spent an enjoyable hour in solitude, relieved that she had finally found a little respite.

A respite that was, unfortunately, soon interrupted.

"My lady?"

Tabitha looked up, a trifle irritated that she had been pulled from her solitude. "Yes?"

The butler came a little further into the room and bowed his head, perhaps sensing her displeasure. "Lord Yarmouth wishes to see you, my lady," he said, as Tabitha swallowed hard, her contentedness fleeing her in an instant. "What are your wishes at present?" Clearly aware that she had expected not to entertain guests this afternoon and was, at least for the moment, tucked up in the library with a book and her tea tray, the butler looked at her hesitantly as though worried she might rail at him for allowing Lord Yarmouth entry in the first place.

Tabitha swallowed hard again, feeling herself grow tense as she placed her book down carefully. "But of course, I will see him," she said quickly, trying to dismiss her own feelings of anxiety. "Thank you, allow him in at once. And fetch whatever he requires to drink."

The butler nodded and retreated, with Lord Yarmouth being shown in only a few seconds later. Tabitha rose from her chair at once, astonished at the way her stomach tightened and her heart began to quicken as he came towards her, his hands outstretched.

"My dear Tabitha," he said, a look in his eyes that she had not seen before. "You left the assembly early last evening, and I did not get the opportunity to speak to you before you were gone."

Tabitha took his hands in her own but did not say a word, finding her throat constricting tightly as she looked up into his eyes. Why had she never noticed before just how captivating they were?

"I spoke harshly to you yesterday, and I am sorry for it," he continued, standing close to her now and searching her face, his hands tightly holding hers. "I practically berated you for something that I had asked you to do, and that was very wrong of me, Tabitha. I only pray that you can forgive me."

Nodding inanely, Tabitha tried to smile but felt her lips stick fast together, refusing to move.

"I can see that I have caused you pain that has not yet left," Lord Yarmouth continued, dropping one of her hands and, much to her astonishment, reaching up to press his hand against her cheek, his eyes now fixing tightly to hers as though he were desperate to convey just how regretful he really was. "I should never have spoken to you in such a manner. It was entirely unfair of me. I want you to know that I am truly grateful for all that you have done."

Forcing air into her lungs, Tabitha drew in a long breath and let it out slowly, aware of the tingling in her skin from where his hand had rested upon her cheek. "I quite understand," she said, stepping to one side and releasing his other hand so that she might resume her seat again. "It was something of a surprise to me also, the way that Lady Sutherland came towards us both. It was not at all what I had expected."

"But it worked out marvelously," Lord Yarmouth declared, beaming at her. "Lady Marina is to accompany me to the theatre tomorrow—along with her mother, of course! I shall be quite the envy of almost every gentleman in London." He tilted his head and studied her for a moment. "I do hope that Miss Bartlett will not be too upset if I set her aside."

Something like anger burst through Tabitha's chest as she studied Lord Yarmouth. "You mean to say," she began, choosing her words with great care and deliberation rather than giving way to all that she wanted to say. "You mean to say that you will no longer give any attention to Miss Bartlett, even though you considered doing so before?"

Lord Yarmouth shrugged. "It is of no great consequence, I am sure. Miss Bartlett was, as you know, someone who was difficult to converse with, even though I sympathized with her situation regarding her mother. But Lady Marina is quite the opposite of Miss Bartlett! She is quite able to converse with me, listens well to what I have to say, and is quite beautiful also." A smile of contentment spread across his face, but this only added to Tabitha's anger. Rising from her chair on unsteady legs, she planted both hands on her hips and glared at him.

"You mean to say that it is Lady Marina's beauty that has captured you rather than any true knowledge of her character?" she said, her voice rising slowly. "I had not expected such shallowness from you, Lord Yarmouth!"

From the expression on his face, Tabitha knew such words surprised him. His smile had shattered, his eyes had flared, and a slight paleness had come into his cheeks, but Tabitha felt no guilt in what she had said. This was just as she saw things, just as she saw *him* to be, and that, in itself, was something of a shock.

"I—I do not know what you mean, Tabitha," Lord Yarmouth said, his voice faltering. "I have been considering Miss Bartlett for some days, as you know, but I do not think that I can permit myself to consider her any further, given what I know of her."

"And when did you come to this decision?" Tabitha asked sharply, her fury like a burning fire that simply grew in strength with every second that passed. "Was it before or after you set eyes on Lady Marina?" Lifting her chin, she saw him flush and drop his gaze and felt disappointment sear her. "For before you saw Lady Marina, I am certain that you spoke to me of Miss Bartlett, stating that you had not seen her as yet and expressing a small amount of dissatisfaction over such a thing. Is that not so?"

Lord Yarmouth opened his mouth to speak, and then, after a moment, let out his breath in a long hiss, running one hand through his hair as he kept his gaze fixed to the floor.

"You may have come to apologize, Lord Yarmouth, but I believe you have done more harm in your visit," she finished, desperate for him to remove himself from her presence. "I have never once thought you vain, hoping that other gentlemen will see the lady on your arm and be filled with jealousy because of it. You have never expressed to me a desire simply to find a lady whose beauty outshines every other, so that you might have *her* as a bride. I had thought better of you than that, Yarmouth." Walking to the door, she yanked it open, heat and rage burning through her veins. "Depart, if you please. I must have some time to think on all of this."

Lord Yarmouth stared at her for a long moment, his mouth having dropped open at her final announcement. It was as though he expected her to change her mind, to slowly close it and state that she had overreacted, but Tabitha remained steadfast. She wanted to be entirely alone, and Lord Yarmouth seemed unable to comprehend that.

"Tabitha," Lord Yarmouth said, taking a step closer to

her, his hand outstretched as he began to frown. "Please, I—"

"I will see you this evening," Tabitha interrupted sharply. "But for the moment, I should like to be alone. There is much I must think on."

Again, Lord Yarmouth simply stared at her in evident astonishment at her reaction, but slowly, as he saw that she was not inclined to change her mind, he began to move away. His head low, he made his way towards the door.

"Tabitha," he said again, pausing just as he came to pass by her, his eyes searching her face. "I—I am sorry."

Tabitha turned her face away from his, finding herself somewhere between wanting to express her fury towards him and wanting to break down into sobs. It was a relief when he left the room and all the more of a relief when she was able to shut the door behind him. Sagging against it, she closed her eyes tightly and felt the anger begin to drain away from her almost at once, leaving a weakness in its place. She had not meant to react with such anger, but it had been within her regardless, sending spikes of ire all through her. Every word she had said to Lord Yarmouth was quite true. She had *never* expected him to speak in such a way, to express such a shallow sentiment about a lady, and yet he had done so without hesitation. There had not even been the opportunity to tell him the truth about Miss Bartlett, but there was no need, evidently, to even mention her name again since he was now set on courting Lady Marina.

Closing her eyes, Tabitha pushed hard against the tears that threatened to flood them. She would *not* permit herself to cry. This was nothing more than foolishness, for what need did *she* have for Lord Yarmouth to behave properly? It was his decision what young lady he chose to wed, and, if that was to be Lady Marina, then what did it matter to her?

Pushing herself away from the door, Tabitha turned to open it, glancing out quickly to make certain that Lord Yarmouth was not waiting for her to emerge, and then quickly returned to her room.

"I am going to take a short walk," she told her maid, who was busy laying out her things for the dinner party later that evening. "I shall not be long."

Quickly, the maid helped her change into her walking dress, and within a few minutes, Tabitha found herself outside, drawing in great lungfuls of air. The walk, she told herself, would do her good. Her anger would fade completely as she walked, her mind would settle as she took in the sights and sounds of London. To remain at home, to pace and cry and grow frustrated with all that had occurred, would do her no good at all. Better to walk outside for a time so that she might grow a little weary, and, in turn, bring a quietness to her mind.

ONE HOUR later and Tabitha was quite exhausted. She had walked much further than she had intended and found herself in a small park where she might rest a while. The difficulty had been that, as she had been walking, her mind had been so busy with all that she had been thinking of that she had not been aware of where her feet were taking her.

Sinking down onto a bench, Tabitha closed her eyes and wished that she could rub her feet. It had, perhaps, been a little foolish to allow her anger to push her so far from home, although, of course, she could simply take a hackney back to her townhouse.

She was not quite ready to return, however. When she did, she would immediately have to make certain she ate something before beginning preparations to go out to the dinner party. The prospect of seeing Lord Yarmouth again was not a pleasant one, and Tabitha knew she would struggle to contain her feelings in proper company.

"Do you mind if I join you?"

Tabitha looked up in surprise, having not even realized that an older lady had approached her. She looked a little tired, and immediately, Tabitha made to rise, but the lady gestured for her to remain seated.

"I am sure there is plenty of space for us both," she said, coming to sit down beside Tabitha with a contented sigh escaping her. "I thought to come out walking this afternoon, but I have walked a little too far."

Tabitha's lips quirked ruefully. "As have I," she said as the lady laughed. "But I shall take a hackney home." She smiled at the lady, aware that she had not yet introduced herself. "And you?"

"I shall do the same," the lady replied, her blue eyes sparkling in the sunshine. "Once I have rested for a time, at least." She studied Tabitha for a moment. "I hope you do not mind, but I must ask—are you quite all right?"

A frown rippled across Tabitha's brow. "What do you mean?"

"Only that you look troubled," the lady replied carefully. "I do not mean to pry, but I should be glad to listen to you if you wish to unburden yourself."

Tabitha tried to laugh, tried to state that it was quite all right and that she was not at all troubled, but neither of her intentions came to fruition. Her laugh died in her throat, and the words she wanted to say refused to come to her lips.

"You may have noticed that I am a little older than you," the lady continued with a small smile. "I do have some wisdom in certain matters. I was married myself but have also lost my husband and many others that were dear to me. I have raised a family of my own, and, these last years, have set to assisting those who have had very little aid from any other quarter." Her head tipped to the left, her eyes assessing Tabitha carefully. "I may not be able to say very much at all, but I would be glad to listen to anything you have to say."

"It is nothing but foolishness on my part," Tabitha found herself saying, unable to prevent herself from speaking to this older lady despite the awareness that she might very well seek to then take whatever Tabitha had said and whisper it to her friends within the *beau monde*. "It is a matter of my own making, in a way. Perhaps I never should have..." She trailed off, looking at the older lady with a sense of wariness beginning to swoop around her. "It does not matter."

"I am very discreet," the lady said softly. "I have

never once whispered a secret that belonged to another, even if I was given permission to do so."

Closing her eyes for a moment, Tabitha shook her head mutely. Hot tears began to burn in her eyes, and she dared not open them for fear that they would fall.

"You are struggling with something great, are you not?" the lady said kindly. "I should be glad to help you."

"It—it is a very dear friend of mine," Tabitha began, tears beginning to roll down her cheeks as she spoke, her eyes fixed to the path before her rather than to the lady, who quickly handed her a handkerchief. "He has asked me to assist him in finding a suitable wife."

The lady nodded slowly. "Tell me how long you have been acquainted with this gentleman," she said. "And has there ever been anything more between you?"

In halting tones, Tabitha managed to express everything about Lord Yarmouth without ever once mentioning his name. She told the lady all about their acquaintance, how it had grown to a very deep friendship, and how she now struggled to become accustomed to the idea of his marrying another.

"I am sure it is because I fear our friendship will change, which is, I know, quite ridiculous," Tabitha said with a sniff. "It will, of course, become different from what it is at present, but that is something that I ought to accept without any great difficulty, is it not?"

The lady smiled gently, her blue eyes crinkling at the corners. "Might it not be, my dear, that you have more of an affection for this gentleman than you realize?"

Tabitha stared at her, her eyes dry from tears as what

felt like a cold wind blew all around her, even though it was a beautifully warm day.

"That is not something that has ever occurred to you before, it seems," the lady continued with a small lift of her mouth on one side. "I may be quite mistaken, my dear, but I believe, from what you have said, that you care very deeply for this particular fellow."

"I—I do not think—"

Unable to finish the sentence, Tabitha looked away from the lady and stared hard at the ground, her breathing rapid and her hands clenched tightly into fists. It could not be! Surely such a thing would have occurred to her at the first? She would have realized that she had a deep affection for Lord Yarmouth that went far beyond that of mere friendship, would she not?

"If you are questioning as to why you were not aware of this particular thing before, might I suggest that it is sometimes only brought to light when a change occurs that steals away the possibility of anything more ever occurring between you." Her expression was gentle, and Tabitha felt no threat from her. Rather, it was as though she had been sent by some sort of divine purpose simply to reveal the truth to Tabitha before disappearing into the ether. "In asking you to seek a bride for him, you slowly have become aware of what you feel for him but, given that you have had nothing but a friendship between you for some time, the possibility of such a thing has not come into your mind. Or mayhap it is that you *cannot* think of it for fear of what might change should you do so."

Swallowing hard, Tabitha closed her eyes and let out a long breath. "I have never once considered the possibility that I might care for him," she said softly. "But now that you have revealed it to me, I find that I can think of nothing else." Lifting her head, she looked at the lady again, aware of the sympathetic expression on her face and finding herself increasingly grateful for her words of wisdom. "It all begins to fall into place now."

"Then I am glad I enquired," the lady replied as Tabitha handed her back her handkerchief. "Oh no, my dear, you keep it." She smiled and rose to her feet. "I suspect there may be a few more tears as you return home."

"Wait!" Tabitha exclaimed, reaching to grasp the lady's arm. "What should I do now?"

The older lady laughed and patted Tabitha's hand. "I cannot tell you what to do next," she replied calmly. "You will have to decide such a thing yourself, for I cannot advise you."

Tabitha let go of the lady's arm and sat back, such tumultuous emotions flooding her that, for a moment, it felt as though she could not breathe. She could barely come to terms with what it was that had been revealed to her at present, much less think of what she was to do next! Suddenly, the thought of seeing Lord Yarmouth again this evening was terrifying, her heart pounding furiously as she imagined what she would feel at seeing him again.

"I cannot thank you enough for all of your help," she said as the lady smiled at her. "Pray, do not say a word to another about what I have said."

"Of course, I will not," the lady replied—and for

whatever reason, Tabitha believed her without a doubt. "I do hope all works out as you hope."

"Thank you," Tabitha said again as the lady smiled and turned to make her way out of the park. "Might I ask your name? I am Lady Croome."

Looking back at her, the lady's eyes twinkled. "Lady Newfield," she replied with a small bobbing curtsy. "Good afternoon, Lady Croome. I do hope that we shall meet again one day soon."

CHAPTER ELEVEN

"I cannot understand it."

Oliver grimaced at his reflection as he ran one finger lightly over his cravat, finally satisfied with his valet's efforts.

"You cannot?" Lord Jennings repeated with a roll of his eyes. "You do not think there to be any truth in what Lady Croome said?"

"Certainly, I do not," Oliver replied, although the moment he said such a thing, a spiral of guilt tore up through him. "She is...I do not know what it is within her that caused her to speak so."

Lord Jennings drained his brandy glass. "She is being quite honest with you, old boy," he said without any sort of malice in his voice. "It is *most* unlike you to consider a lady on her appearance alone." Setting his glass down, he rose to his feet. "You have always been a gentleman who has never been caught by a pair of beautiful eyes, or a coy smile. In fact, I believe that you have shunned such young ladies before, believing that there is no substance to them and that, therefore, they are not worthy of your time." One eyebrow lifted. "But now, it seems, you are so taken with Lady Marina, based solely on appearance, that you have instantly forgotten about Miss Bartlett."

Oliver grimaced, trying to find some sort of excuse that would satisfy not only Lord Jennings, but also the guilt that rushed through him. The truth was that everything Lord Jennings said was fair, for Oliver had never once considered a lady based solely on her outward appearance but, then again, he told himself, he had never thought of courting a lady before. Not with any seriousness, at least.

"I have never thought of courtship before," he told Lord Jennings, satisfying himself with his answer. "I must think of all that I require in a wife."

"And you require someone with as much beauty as Lady Marina?" Lord Jennings replied, a touch of sarcasm in his words. "I am quite certain you informed me that Miss Bartlett was very lovely in appearance, even if she was quiet and difficult to engage in conversation. You stated that you thought you should continue with your acquaintance with her for a time before making any real decision about the lady."

"That was before I met Lady Marina," Oliver retorted sharply. "And she is a good deal easier to converse with than Miss Bartlett. I do not have to make a great amount of effort when it comes to Lady Marina. Surely that should be enough to—"

"And just how many conversations have you had

with Lady Marina?" Lord Jennings interrupted, now appearing a little irritated. "You have not yet taken the lady to the theatre, from what I recall, and thus you must have only spoken with her last evening."

Lifting his chin, Oliver tried to find something to say in response to this, something that would put Lord Jennings in his place, but to his own chagrin, nothing came to mind.

"You have only spoken to her the once, then," Lord Jennings said with a shake of head. "And that is certainly not enough for a gentleman to make up his mind about any acquaintance, be it lady or gentleman. No, it is precisely as Lady Croome says, and it is little wonder that she is upset." His jaw set, and he studied Oliver with a hard gaze. "I think you have made a foolish decision, Yarmouth. It is just as well Miss Bartlett has eloped, else you might have had more than one lady to placate."

Oliver frowned, about to make some sort of retort only to find himself astonished to hear of Miss Bartlett.

"You had not heard she has eloped," Lord Jennings said, looking at Oliver steadily. "Yes, she has eloped. Lady Ashbrook and Lady Croome told me of it last evening. I believe Lady Croome gave Miss Bartlett her carriage to take to Scotland."

"I do not understand," Oliver replied, now all the more confused. "If Lady Croome knew that Miss Bartlett intended to elope, then why did she even present Miss Bartlett to me in the first place?" He threw up his hands, ignoring Lord Jennings' explanation entirely and speaking over his words. "She cannot be angry with me regarding Lady Marina if she assisted Miss Bartlett in escaping from not only myself, but from London! That is not to be tolerated!"

"Now, wait a moment!" Lord Jennings exclaimed, but Oliver shook his head, striding towards the door.

"I do not need your explanations," he said, pulling the door open and fixing Lord Jennings with a glare. "I am very well capable of speaking to Lady Croome myself, given that I shall be in her company this evening. No, I shall have no further excuses, Lord Jennings. Lady Croome is the one who must explain her actions. I shall hear no words from you."

THE MOMENT OLIVER was shown into the drawing-room, he began to search for Lady Croome, his eyes roving over each and every guest as he nodded and tried to smile at the others present. Unfortunately, he was forced to speak to one or two others before he could make his way through the room, finding each conversation difficult to maintain given his determination to find Lady Croome. There was a small fire burning within his heart, an unsettling anger that threatened to overcome him entirely if he did not give vent to it soon. He could not understand why Lady Croome had, first of all, suggested Miss Bartlett to him if she knew she intended to elope, and, secondly, why she had assisted the lady in doing so! She could not hold any anger towards him when *she* had been the one to encourage and assist Miss Bartlett to marry another. She should be relieved that he had thought of Lady Marina rather than Miss Bartlett, instead of speaking with such harshness!

Finally, his eyes settled upon her. She was standing near the back of the room, conversing with one Lady Pettigrew. Oliver approached carefully, making certain not to be too obvious with his desire to speak to her. Instead, he waited patiently until Lady Pettigrew had stepped away before hurrying forward, seeing something flare in Lady Croome's eyes as he approached.

"Lord Yarmouth," Lady Croome murmured, a flush of red warming her cheeks as she looked up at him. "Good evening."

He did not even greet her in response. "I hear Miss Bartlett has eloped."

Lady Croome looked surprised but then nodded. "I was to tell you so last evening, but there was no opportunity," she said in a manner that suggested it was not at all important. "I am glad you have heard of it, however. I presume Lord Jennings told you?"

Oliver could hardly believe just how nonchalant she was being. "You encouraged me towards a lady that had every intention of eloping?" he said, his brows lifting as he saw a flicker of a frown cross her forehead. "And then, not only did you assist her with that endeavor, you then expressed frustration towards me when I spoke to you about my intentions to forget Miss Bartlett and instead turn my attention to Lady Marina!"

The change that took place in Lady Croome's face was marked. The color drained from her face, her lips set into a firm, hard line, and her brows fell hard over her eyes.

"I have not been lackadaisical in my approach when it comes to assisting you with this, Yarmouth," she said, keeping her voice low but her words so forceful that they hit him like sharp darts. "I did not know that Miss Bartlett intended to elope before I suggested her to you," she continued, a spot of color beginning to reveal itself in her cheeks. "I came upon her in the gardens with her particular gentleman and, such was her distress that I could not simply refuse to help her! If you recall, Yarmouth, I *was* attempting to speak to you of it last evening before we were interrupted by Lady Sutherland."

One eyebrow arched, and she waited for him to respond, but Oliver found himself struggling to remember what she spoke of. This made Lady Croome shake her head with either exasperation or frustration, and she closed her eyes for a moment, drawing in a long breath, which, he presumed, was to assist her in keeping her temper. He did not know what to feel at this moment, his anger still burning through him but slowly beginning to remove itself from him as Lady Croome continued to explain.

"I remain frustrated with you for the way you spoke of Lady Marina," she continued, opening her eyes. "I have never known you to remark upon a lady's outward appearance and to hold onto it with such eagerness. Nor have I heard you mention how other gentlemen will be envious of your position." Her brow furrowed, and she looked up at him steadily as though she were seeing him for the very first time. "I thought I knew you very well,

Yarmouth. Perhaps, through this, I have discovered I am wrong."

Oliver swallowed hard. Her explanation for why she had encouraged Miss Bartlett towards him only for her to then go on to elope was, he considered, quite understandable. If she had not known, then it was quite reasonable for her to have suggested the lady. Assisting Miss Bartlett in her elopement was something he would have expected from Lady Croome, truth be told, for that kindness of heart and compassionate spirit was something he had long admired.

"I shall do nothing more for you in this regard," Lady Croome said, her eyes now sparkling with unshed tears and her voice breaking with emotion. "If Lady Marina does not suit, then my fourth lady was to be Miss Phoebe Morgan, who is the daughter of Viscount Jamieson. I hope, Yarmouth, that you find one of these two ladies to be suitable, for perhaps then, I shall not feel as though I have failed entirely."

"Tabitha." Oliver closed his eyes, wishing that he could retreat from the room and begin his entry all over again. He had spoken foolishly and without consideration, letting his anger lead him rather than consider whether or not there might be a reasonable explanation to what had occurred. "I—I am sorry."

When he opened his eyes, Lady Croome was dabbing at her eyes with her handkerchief, clearly trying to restore her own composure. When she lifted her head to look at him again, her eyes were clear, and, aside from a small sniff, she appeared to be quite herself.

"This does not mean that we shall not remain friends,

Yarmouth," she said quietly. "Although, mayhap, it shall begin to open up a chasm between us that will permit us to, slowly, reduce our friendship to a mere acquaintance."

Her words tore at his heart. "That is what you wish?" he croaked, his heart now thudding painfully. "That is what you want from me?"

She shook her head, but a sad smile lifted one side of her mouth. "It is what must happen, Yarmouth. Do you not see? You are to be engaged and then wed to which-ever lady you choose. Things cannot remain the same between us. It would be both improper and unfeeling towards the lady you choose to be your wife." Blinking rapidly, the thought evidently causing her tears to return, Lady Croome cleared her throat and then lifted her chin a notch. "I wish you well with Lady Marina tomorrow, Yarmouth. Now, if you will excuse me."

Oliver could do nothing but step aside, allowing Lady Croome to move past him. She wound her way quickly towards Lady Ashbrook whilst he remained precisely where he was, both ashamed of his own callous behavior and horrified at what she had told him. To be separated from Lady Croome? To never again have the closeness that they presently enjoyed? That could not satisfy him, and neither, surely, could it satisfy the lady.

But is she correct?

Closing his eyes again, Oliver drew in a long breath and tried to quieten his thumping heart and whirling thoughts. He needed to apologize to her, to let her know the depths of his guilt and shame that now overpowered him. And yet the thought of going to her only to know that there was this chasm breaking the ground between them filled him with dread. He did not want such a thing to occur. He could not even dream of being apart from Lady Croome in such a way, to no longer have the friendship and intimacy that they had, for so long, enjoyed.

"Is something the matter?"

Opening his eyes quickly and trying his best to put a smile onto his face, Oliver saw none other than Lord Jennings looking back at him, an air of concern about him.

"I saw Lady Croome speaking with you," Lord Jennings continued, turning slightly in the direction she had gone. "And then you appeared distraught." His brow lifted, although there was no trace of malice in his voice. "Things did not go particularly well, I gather."

Oliver groaned quietly, trying not to attract the attention of the other guests and being all too aware that the dinner gong would soon be rung. "I should not have been as absurd as I was, Jennings," he muttered, a deep sense of shame beginning to crawl over his skin. "I should have allowed you to explain." Taking in a deep breath, he turned his gaze to his friend. "She stated that our friendship cannot continue, but that cannot be the case, surely?"

To his horror, Lord Jennings did not immediately disagree. Instead, his lips pursed, and lines formed across his brow.

"You surely cannot expect for your acquaintance with Lady Croome to continue just as it is at present once you are a married gentleman," he said slowly, his eyes a little narrowed as though trying to assess whether or not this was, in fact, what Oliver thought. "She is quite correct in making such remarks."

This brought even more pain to Oliver's heart, his lips pulling into a tight line as his mind struggled to accept what he now knew to be true. Why had he never considered such a thing before? For whatever reason, he had expected things to remain just the same regardless of whether he was engaged or married. He had never once thought of it...or had it been that he had simply *refused* to think of it?

"That is the dinner gong," Lord Jennings remarked, shaking Oliver out of his thoughts. "Come now; you must not think of such a thing at present, for appearance's sake at least."

"Of course, of course," Oliver muttered, giving himself a slight shake and trying his utmost to appear just as nonchalant as possible, despite the fact that he was greatly troubled by what had been said. "You are quite right."

"You can speak to Lady Croome at a later time— tomorrow, perhaps," Lord Jennings continued as the guests began to stand together so that they might walk through for dinner. "Leave your thoughts for the present. It will do you no good to continue to consider them this evening."

Oliver nodded and came to join the others, but, try as he might, he could not help but think on Lady Croome. They had become very dear friends these last few years, and the thought of being separated from her was almost more than he could bear. Sitting down mechanically at the table, his gaze immediately found Lady Croome and, as the first course was served, Oliver could not remove his eyes from her.

Can this truly be? he asked himself, seeing how she glanced at him before looking away, a hint of color in her face. *And why is it that I simply cannot accept it without difficulty?"*

❧

"Right this way, Lady Marina."

Oliver smiled warmly as Lady Marina and Lady Sutherland stepped towards his private box. Their evening had, thus far, gone without particular difficulty. Oliver had arrived to collect them both and had only had to wait for a short time until they had both been ready. Lady Sutherland was dressed in a dark and somewhat drab gown, whereas Lady Marion was resplendent in a gown of light blue, which brought his attention to her eyes. Everything about her was graceful and delicate, and Oliver had to admit that there was a sense of pride deep within him that came with having Lady Marion in his company.

"I confess I do not even know what the performance is to be this evening," Lady Marina said, sitting down carefully as a shade of pink settled into her cheeks, her smile a little uncertain.

"It is to be an opera," Oliver said, quickly explaining what the story was to be. "I have heard it is quite excellent." He glanced all about him, fully aware that most of those who attended the theatre came solely to see who else was present as well as to ensure that they themselves were seen. What would they think of Lady Marina's presence this evening? Would rumors begin to fly throughout the *beau monde* about his attentions towards her? Was that something he wanted?

"I am very glad to be present with you, Lord Yarmouth," Lady Marina said, although Oliver detected no warmth in her voice, nor was there even a flicker of a smile. "Thank you for your generous invitation."

Oliver smiled but glanced towards Lady Sutherland rather than speaking to Lady Marina. He was not at all surprised to see her giving a small nod to her daughter, her lips curving and her eyes bright with a satisfied expression.

The words from Lady Marina were not genuine, then. They did not come from within her own heart nor from any true sense of appreciation. It was all rehearsed, just as the lines were practiced and then performed by the actors this evening.

His heart sank.

"Ah, it seems we are to begin!" Lady Sutherland exclaimed as someone strode out from the wings into the middle of the stage. "An opera is one of my very great pleasures, Lord Yarmouth, just as it is my daughter's. Is that not so, Marina?"

It took a fraction of a second for the lady to respond.

"Yes, yes, of course," she said, hastily, looking up at Oliver with wide eyes. "It is the most enjoyable of all performances, in my consideration."

Oliver smiled back at her but did not feel any true delight. It seemed that Lady Marina was only giving the answers her mother had deemed appropriate. It was, in fact, that the daughter was being controlled in her responses by her mother, forced to speak only the words that came from Lady Sutherland rather than from her own considerations. He turned his face directly towards the stage rather than continuing to look at Lady Marina. There was no delight in her company now. It was as though Lady Marina were afraid to speak or act in any way other than the way that Lady Sutherland accepted. Would she continue to behave in such a fashion if he were to court her? And if they were to marry? Would she then act in such a way, looking only to say what *he* would think acceptable?

As the music began, Oliver's mind returned to Lady Croome. She was a lady who knew her own mind. She was honest with him always, although gentle in all that she said. It was to his own shame that he had spoken with harshness and cruelty towards Lady Croome when she had only told him the truth. Would he prefer a lady who spoke nothing but what he wanted to hear? Or did he wish for a lady who would tell him the truth, regardless of how it might make him feel?

A rueful smile tugged at his lips. It was not something he needed to consider, for the answer was already right before him. Even though he had not reacted well to Lady Croome's candor, he knew it was something that he had needed to hear. He would much rather have a wife who spoke the truth to him at all times rather than remain silent for fear of speaking out of turn.

Then what are you to do? he asked himself as his brow furrowed. *Are you to continue with Lady Marina? Court her in the hope that she might become as honest and as open as Lady Croome?*

Shaking his head to himself, Oliver sat back in his chair and took in a long breath. It was clear enough to him that such an acquaintance would not be one that he could continue, but what he was to do next, Oliver was quite unsure. The answer, it seemed, was not yet to reveal itself.

CHAPTER TWELVE

Tabitha picked up her teacup and took a small sip. "You are not telling me the truth."

Sighing quietly, Tabitha looked at her friend. "I have nothing further to say on the matter, Dinah," she said quietly. "I have brought an end to my…" She tilted her head, trying to find the correct word. "My responsibilities regarding Lord Yarmouth. Therefore, I shall do nothing further to assist him, and he will make his own decision regarding whether either of the final two ladies I have suggested is suitable."

Lady Ashbrook shook her head, a clear amount of exasperation written in her expression. "I know that you are not telling me everything that occurred," she said firmly. "I am one of your closest friends, and I was very well aware that, during the dinner party, there was a great deal of tension between yourself and Lord Yarmouth. He could not seem to remove his gaze from you, and you, in return, did all you could to look away from him!"

Tabitha tried her best to remain calm and quite

composed but could not prevent tears from beginning to cloud her vision. The truth was that ever since the dinner party, she had been torn apart with all manner of emotions as regarded Lord Yarmouth. The realization that she herself was deeply in love with Lord Yarmouth had been entirely overwhelming, and when she had seen him walking into the drawing-room at Lady Ashbrook's, her heart had begun to pound with such fury that she had hardly been able to breathe.

And then, he had spoken to her with such anger, such distrust, that she had felt her heart tear into pieces. It had taken all of her strength to remain composed, to tell him that she would no longer assist him with his endeavors in finding a wife. She had given him the name of the fourth lady she had considered and had then stepped away, unable to speak another word to him. Lady Ashbrook was quite correct—she had done nothing other than avoid Lord Yarmouth's gaze for the rest of the evening, whilst being fully aware that he was doing nothing other than watching her.

"Tabitha." Lady Ashbrook leaned forward in her chair and fixed Tabitha with a steady gaze. "What is the matter? I can tell that you are greatly troubled, but you will do no good remaining here, quiet and alone with your thoughts."

Tabitha tried to speak, tried to give some sort of explanation, but instead felt tears begin to warm her cheeks. Closing her eyes tightly, she pulled her handkerchief to wipe them away, but more and more came.

"Tabitha!" Lady Ashbrook exclaimed, hurrying

towards her, bending down in front of Tabitha's chair. "I did not mean to upset you. I am sorry if—"

"I do not want Lord Yarmouth to find a wife!" Tabitha exclaimed, opening her eyes to look desperately into Lady Ashbrook's face. "*I* should be that lady, should I not? *I* should be the one to wed him, not any other."

In an instant, Lady Ashbrook's expression changed from concern to utter astonishment.

"I love him desperately," Tabitha cried, unable to keep what she felt in her heart any longer. "It has become more and more of a struggle to keep myself contained when choosing such young ladies for him to consider. I did not even *realize* that I felt this way until I spoke to a particular lady who pointed it out to me. And now, I feel so utterly distraught that I—"

"Oh, my dear!" Lady Ashbrook interrupted, flinging her arms around Tabitha, who simply could not contain her sobs. "I am so very sorry that you have come to realize this now! I had hoped that it would be apparent to you much sooner than this moment but, given that nothing had been said by either yourself or Lord Yarmouth, I thought that perhaps I had been mistaken."

It took a few minutes for Tabitha to regain her composure enough to speak. She drew back from Lady Ashbrook's embrace, and, sniffing in a most unladylike manner, wiped her eyes with her damp handkerchief. Lady Ashbrook sank into a seat next to her, her gaze trained on Tabitha as she studied her with concern.

"You—you knew that I cared for Lord Yarmouth?" she whispered as Lady Ashbrook smiled gently. "Why did you not say?"

"I did not know for certain," Lady Ashbrook said gently. "Lord Jennings and I have considered it together, and we were not at all certain as to whether or not we were correct." Her head tilted to one side. "Therefore, we chose not to say anything in particular."

Tabitha closed her eyes and drew in a long breath, doing her best not to say a single word as she let what Lady Ashbrook had said run through her mind.

"Lord Jennings is quite convinced that Lord Yarmouth is also in love with you, Tabitha," Lady Ashbrook continued quietly. "I think you should speak to him."

Tabitha shook her head. "I cannot."

"You *must!*" Lady Ashbrook exclaimed, a fresh light shining in her eyes. "If you reveal your heart to him, then I am sure that he will come to realize the very same thing."

Remembering how he had spoken to her, how he had blamed her, Tabitha shook her head. "I fear that he thinks poorly of me at present," she said slowly. "Besides which, I have already stated that things must change between us."

Lady Ashbrook looked at her, confused. "In what way?"

"I stated," Tabitha replied, her heart beginning to ache within her, "that we could no longer be as we have been. That our friendship must begin to change, that we must begin to separate—simply because he is to be wed, of course." Tears came into her eyes again, but she forced them back, blinking furiously. "I fear that I must give way now to whichever of the ladies he chooses. It is the right path to take, Dinah, yet I fear doing so."

Lady Ashbrook drew in a long breath and then let it out slowly, giving Tabitha the impression that she was thinking about what ought to be done next. Tabitha, however, was quite convinced that there was nothing more she could do. She had explained things very clearly to Lord Yarmouth, had stated that they must now begin to step away from each other and could not now simply return to him and state that she was, in fact, desperate to wed him instead of either Lady Marina or Miss Morgan, should he choose to seek that particular lady out.

"Besides," Tabitha found herself saying hopelessly, "I am not at all the sort of lady Lord Yarmouth would seek for a bride." Her shoulders slumped. "Do you not recall that I told you I knew him well enough to know precisely the sort of young lady he would choose?" Again, tears came to her eyes, and this time, she let them fall. "I have no dowry. I have no great fortune. I live carefully and can only come to London due to the charity of others." She began to dab at her eyes again, her voice shaking. "I do not possess the beauty that he seeks."

"You are *very* lovely, Tabitha!" Lady Ashbrook broke in, but Tabitha, recalling how Lord Yarmouth had reacted when he had seen Lady Marina for the first time, gave a sad shake of her head.

"I know full well that he is partial to fair hair and green eyes," she said sorrowfully. "And what do I have but the opposite?" Sadly, she gestured to her dark hair and brown eyes. "You are kind to pay me such a compliment, Dinah, but it is not what Lord Yarmouth seeks."

Lady Ashbrook drew herself up. "Now that, I know, is nothing more than nonsense," she stated firmly. "You are very beautiful indeed, and I am *certain* that Lord Yarmouth thinks so also. Besides which, he knows of your character and of your integrity, my dear Tabitha, and that, I am certain, will draw him all the more towards you. Do you not think that he feels as much pain as you when it comes to the realization that he shall soon have to part from you, to pull away from the friendship that has sustained you both for so long? Do you believe that he can simply accept such a thing without hesitation?"

Recalling how confused Lord Yarmouth had been at her statement that they could no longer remain as close as they had been, Tabitha allowed herself a small shrug. "I think it has not occurred to him before," she answered honestly, wiping her eyes. "Perhaps, like me, he simply thought that all could go on as we had intended. I do not think he had ever truly considered what would have to change. But I have made it clear, and, since then, he has not written nor called." Her throat constricted, and she dabbed at her eyes. "In fact, I have heard that he was out with Lady Marina at the theatre, just as they had planned. That does not speak of heartbreak, of difficulty or trial. Therefore," she finished, taking in a deep breath and trying her best to clear her vision of tears, "I shall soon remove myself from London and pray that Lord Yarmouth finds himself a suitable bride."

This, however, did not satisfy Lady Ashbrook, for she immediately began to frown and shake her head, muttering something under her breath as she did so. Rising from her chair, she began to pace back and forth in the room, leaving Tabitha to watch her do so as she herself finished wiping her eyes, determined not to cry anymore.

"No, this will not do," Lady Ashbrook declared firmly, turning on her heel and fixing Tabitha with a determined gaze. "I shall not permit it to be so!"

"What do you—"

Tabitha's question was held back by Lady Ashbrook, who held out one finger and pointed it towards her. "You care for Lord Yarmouth, and both I and Lord Jennings are quite certain that he cares for you also, even if he is not aware of it as yet. Therefore, we must do for you what has been done for him, so that what you feel at present also enters his own heart."

Tabitha closed her eyes for a moment, wishing desperately that she had not said a word to Lady Ashbrook, but, in the same moment, feeling a deep sense of relief that she *had* done so. "I—I do not want anything further to occur, Dinah," she said slowly. "It is entirely up to Lord Yarmouth as to whether or not he returns to my company and as yet—"

"Nonsense," Lady Ashbrook said briskly. "It took someone stating to you that you were in love with Lord Yarmouth for you to realize it, did it not?" She arched one eyebrow and looked steadily at Tabitha until she finally nodded her head, recalling how Lady Newfield had spoken those quiet words that had burned into her soul with such fierceness that it had stolen her very breath. "Then why should Lord Yarmouth not be just as you were?" Coming closer to Tabitha, she bent down and took her hand, smiling into her eyes. "Besides which, do you not want to make certain that you have grasped a hold of every opportunity? Do you truly wish to simply return home without having made every attempt to gain the happiness that you believe, at present, is so far out of your reach?"

Tabitha took in a shaking breath. The possibility of Lord Yarmouth coming to care for her was so small in her own consideration, but she could not deny that there was still a tiny, desperate hope that burned within her heart. A hope that, if she gave consideration to it, might begin to burn with a great and furious fire.

But did she want that? If it were to take a hold of her, then was her heartbreak not to be all the worse if Lord Yarmouth did not turn to her as she hoped? It would certainly mean that they could no longer have any semblance of friendship between them, for she would find it all the more difficult to look to him and his wife without feeling the agony of heartbreak.

But it was an opportunity she could not help but take.

"What is it I must do?" she asked as Lady Ashbrook beamed in delight. "How am I to do what you suggest?"

"It is quite simple!" Lady Ashbrook laughed, rising to her feet again and then making her way back to her own chair. "We shall have Lord Jennings tell Lord Yarmouth that he intends to court you and that you, evidently, have given him your consent."

Tabitha blinked rapidly, staring at Lady Ashbrook as though she had quite lost her senses. "Lord Jennings?" she repeated doubtfully as Lady Ashbrook nodded. "Surely, he would not be open to even the suggestion of matrimony! He is quite disinclined towards such a thing."

"He will be convincing enough," Lady Ashbrook said firmly, making Tabitha wonder whether or not such a thing had been discussed between Lady Ashbrook and Lord Jennings before this moment. "Lord Yarmouth will feel the same as you have felt, realizing that there will be an impasse between you should he choose to marry another and should you marry Lord Jennings. It will be enough to force him to study his own heart, Tabitha, I am quite certain of it."

Tabitha closed her eyes and tried to ignite the hope that was barely flickering in her heart. It was the only opportunity she would have, it seemed, and if Lord Jennings was also determined, then she could not turn away.

"Very well," she said slowly, hearing Lady Ashbrook's exclamation of both approval and delight. "But if it does not give the expected results, then I *shall* leave London, Dinah. I shall return home and await news of Lord Yarmouth's engagement. I shall not be convinced to do or to attempt anything further." She lifted her gaze and fixed it to her friend, seeing how the smile faded from Lady Ashbrook's expression and how it became grave as she nodded slowly.

"I understand," Lady Ashbrook answered gently. "But I believe that you shall find the happiness you barely dare to hope for, Tabitha. Trust me. In a few days, you will have Lord Yarmouth banging at your door, desperate to come and speak to you, frantic with the worry that you shall engage yourself to Lord Jennings before you have the opportunity to speak to him and to hear what is in his heart." Her smile began to return. "And I am determined to be the first to congratulate you both on your engagement."

"I dare not even allow myself to hope for it," Tabitha replied, not allowing her mind to make its way to such a prospect but rather forcing her thoughts to remain in the present. "But it is as you say, Dinah. I must take this opportunity before I return home, just to be quite certain that my feelings are not returned as I hope."

"Or to discover that they *are* returned," Lady Ashbrook added, refusing to allow Tabitha to linger in the negative. "Be brave and bold, my dear friend. It will be worth it in the end."

CHAPTER THIRTEEN

Oliver read the short note for what was now the fifth time, finding himself entirely disinclined towards replying. Lady Marina was very beautiful indeed, but he had found her quite lacking the more he had come to realize just how much she relied on—or was under the control of—her mother.

"Lord Jennings, my lord."

Oliver looked up from his desk to see Lord Jennings strolling into the room, his brows lifted in silent question.

"Yes, yes, I am almost prepared," Oliver said with a sigh. "Where are we to go? Into town?"

"For a short stroll, mayhap?" Lord Jennings suggested, gesturing with one hand towards the sunshine that was pouring through the window. "It is a very fine day, and I have intentions of meeting with a lady that I have decided to court."

The letter fluttered from Oliver's fingers, and he stared openly at Lord Jennings, his jaw slack as the question as to whether or not his friend was being quite serious in his words flung itself into his mind.

Lord Jennings chuckled. "I see that you do not believe me," he said with a grin. "Yet, I can assure you that I have given it a great deal of thought and have decided that this particular lady will suit me very well."

"I—I can hardly believe I am hearing such words from you," Oliver replied, shaking his head and blinking rapidly as Lord Jennings chuckled. "I suppose that I should wish you well, but the truth is I am such a state of confusion! How long have you felt this way?"

Lord Jennings tilted his head, his eyes roving around the room as he considered. And then, he shrugged. "I cannot say particularly," he replied, quietly, "but certainly, these last few days, I have begun to think much more seriously about it all. Perhaps it is because you yourself have been forced into considering matrimony that I have found my own thoughts pulled there also." He shrugged. "As I have said, I cannot quite say."

Oliver did not know how to respond to this, blinking quickly in order to mask his surprise. "Then I hope she accepts you," he said, wondering which of the young ladies that Lord Jennings was acquainted with was the one he had considered. "And you say she will be in town?"

Lord Jennings grinned, his eyes bright. "I believe so, yes," he replied with a wave of his hand towards the door. "As is, I think, that particular young lady, Lady Marina." His eyes danced. "I passed her and her mother walking by the shops as I came here."

"On that point, I fear I must disappoint you," Oliver

replied with a shake of his head. "Lady Marina is not someone I have any intention of marrying."

A look of surprise settled on Lord Jennings' face as he looked enquiringly back at Oliver, who then felt the need to explain a little further.

"Whenever I spoke to the lady, whenever I asked her a question, it was always the words of Lady Sutherland she spoke rather than permitting herself to speak her own thoughts," he explained as Lord Jennings' surprised expression remained fixed to his face. "Such a character-istic is not one that I can find in any way acceptable."

"Because you relish honesty in a lady?" Lord Jennings asked, a hint of disbelief in his voice. "After the way Lady Croome spoke to you, I would have thought that you would have been glad of such a trait in a prospective wife."

Heat climbed into Oliver's face, but he did not turn away from the question. "I was wrong in how I spoke to Lady Croome," he said, aware of the fresh stab of pain that laced his heart as he spoke. "I should not have done so. I should have listened carefully and permitted her to explain before I spoke harshly."

"Yes," Lord Jennings interrupted before Oliver could say more. "Yes, you should have done so. I quite agree." He spread his hands. "What have you done to make amends?"

"To Lady Croome?" Oliver replied, feeling as though a hand was squeezing hard at his heart. "As yet, I have done nothing."

Lord Jennings' eyes flared, his hands falling to his sides. "And why ever not?"

Oliver did not know quite how to respond. Should he say that he had been struggling with all manner of thoughts and emotions as regarded Lady Croome? Ought he to explain that there was something within his heart that could no longer be satisfied with the simple friendship between himself and the lady? That he had found himself comparing Lady Marina to Lady Croome and finding the first lacking in almost every way?

"I—I have not known what to say," he lied, deciding that it was best not to express such deep feelings. "I will, of course, write to her. But I must also write to Lady Marina to make it quite plain that there will be no further meetings between us."

Lord Jennings chuckled but did not ask Oliver anything further about Lady Croome. "Very well," he replied, making his way to a large, overstuffed chair. "Then, I shall sit here and drink your whisky until you write both letters to both ladies so that you are not encumbered with such particular thoughts when we make our way into town."

"On the contrary," Oliver replied, setting the note from Lady Marina down firmly. "We shall go to the bookshop, the park, or wherever you might wish *before* I write such letters." His lips quirked. "I fear that I shall be much too long at these letters otherwise and that it will be morning before I am quite ready to depart!"

This made Lord Jennings laugh, and he rose from the chair he had only just seated himself in and quickly made his way towards the door.

"Then there is no time to waste," he replied as Oliver

followed after him. "To the busy London streets, we shall go!"

～

PERHAPS, Oliver considered, it had been a mistake to come out into the heart of London without having written his note to Lady Marina. Lord Jennings, it seemed, had been quite correct, for his mind was still filled with thoughts of the lady as questions rose within him as to quite how he was to remove himself from her company in as gentle a manner as possible. It was more than obvious that Lady Sutherland was eager for the match, but Oliver knew he could not even consider marrying Lady Marina. There was nothing in her that could satisfy him.

Not when you continually compare her to Lady Croome.

Giving himself a slight shake, Oliver waited until Lord Jennings had alighted from the carriage before following his friend out. Taking in a deep breath, he looked all around him, seeing the hustle and bustle of the streets—and knowing full well that many had come simply to take note of who was out busying themselves in company rather than having any intention of purchasing something new from one of the shops. Oliver could not blame them for doing so, given that he and Lord Jennings were doing precisely that.

"That is interesting now," Lord Jennings murmured, elbowing Oliver none too gently and practically forcing his attention forward. "If you wish it, Yarmouth, I shall introduce you to the fourth lady that was suggested by Lady Croome."

Oliver's heart dropped to his toes. "Indeed," he murmured, wondering whether he ought to pretend to have some sort of interest rather than stating aloud that he was much too preoccupied with his own thoughts as regarded Lady Croome to even consider anyone else. "You know the lady?" Struggling to recall the name Lady Croome had given him, he squeezed his eyes shut for a few moments. "A Miss Martin, was it not?"

Tutting, Lord Jennings eyed him with a disbelieving look. "Lady Croome was correct to state that you were much too preoccupied with Lady Marina's beauty, Yarmouth," he said as though this was the explanation for Oliver's distraction. "It is a Miss Phoebe *Morgan,* and yes, I am acquainted with her. I should be very glad to introduce you if you would like?"

Still not quite sure what to say, Oliver made a non-committal sound in the back of his throat, leaving Lord Jennings frowning. A little embarrassed, Oliver shrugged. "Where is she?"

"She is standing there, with the tall, robust lady beside her, speaking to two young ladies and their chaperone," Lord Jennings said, indicating them with a nod of his head in one particular direction. "Miss Morgan has gold curls escaping from her bonnet and is wearing a gown of light green."

Oliver saw her in a moment. She was, of course, very lovely to look at, but there was nothing within him that leaped at the sight of her.

"You wish to be introduced?" Lord Jennings asked, beginning to move away. "I am sure that she will be—"

"Not so hasty, if you please," Oliver interrupted as Lord Jennings stopped dead. "It is kind of you to offer, but I shall not be seeking any particular introduction to her as yet, Jennings."

"No?" Lord Jennings lifted an eyebrow. "And why might that be? I thought that you had quite set aside Lady Marina. Are you not now looking for someone new?"

Oliver adjusted his hat and cleared his throat, giving him time to come up with an answer that would, he hoped, satisfy Lord Jennings.

"I am a little weary of introductions and the like," he said, hoping that such a justification would make sense to his friend. "It has all come about quickly, and my mind is still heavy with what I must say to Lady Marina. Once I have written a note to her and settled things between us, then, mayhap, I should be glad to meet Miss Morgan."

Holding his breath, he shrugged and prayed that Lord Jennings would not question the matter further, which, thankfully, he did not.

"Very well," Lord Jennings said with a smile that Oliver did not quite understand. "Then shall we take a short walk? I am, as you know, hoping to meet with the lady I have settled my intentions upon for I am sure she informed me that she would be present here this afternoon."

Oliver chuckled, relief spreading through his chest as he turned and began to walk away from Miss Morgan rather than towards her. "And does this poor lady know that you have 'settled your intentions' on her?" he asked as Lord Jennings chuckled. "Or is it something that she has yet to discover?"

"The latter, unfortunately," Lord Jennings replied with a grin. "But it does not matter. We are well acquainted, and I must hope that our acquaintance will put her in mind to accept me."

Not quite certain which particular lady this could be, Oliver kept his judgments to himself and instead continued to walk quietly through the London streets, his gaze meandering along the shop windows without any intention of stopping or purchasing anything of the goods displayed there. It was surprising to hear Lord Jennings speak of such a thing as matrimony given just how determined he had been *not* to do so, but in a way, Oliver was glad that his friend was now considering it. Quietly, Oliver considered it a good thing that Lord Jennings wed. His friend required a few years at his estate, settling into a life of contentment with his wife and, most likely, producing the first of his children, just so long as he was contented with whichever lady he chose to wed! Disinterest would only lead to disaster.

"Good afternoon, Lady Ashbrook!"

"Good afternoon," came the quick reply as Oliver lifted his gaze to see not only Lady Ashbrook approaching them, but also Lady Croome. His stomach twisted, sending a spasm through him that momentarily removed his ability to either speak or move.

She was coming closer but, whilst she gave him a glance, quickly returned her gaze to Lord Jennings. Evidently, Lord Jennings was the one she intended to greet first, already putting distance between them as she had said.

"Good afternoon, Lord Jennings," Lady Croome murmured before shooting another glance towards him. "And to you, Lord Yarmouth."

There was such a strange tension between them that Oliver wanted to reach out and give Lady Croome a shake in the hope of dislodging it somewhat. Instead, he merely cleared his throat and, to his very great relief, managed to greet both ladies without much difficulty.

"Now, where are you headed this fine afternoon?" Lord Jennings asked, his tone eager and his expression bright. "Have you come to look in a shop or two? Or do you intend to take a walk somewhere? Or perhaps Gunter's?"

Oliver frowned as Lady Ashbrook laughed and began to explain their intentions. His friend appeared very eager indeed to know where both ladies were going this afternoon, whereas prior to this, he had been glad of their company but never overly eager to seek it out.

"We thought perhaps to go to Gunter's," Lady Croome clarified once Lady Ashbrook had finished explaining that they had already purchased their intended items. "Or to take a short stroll somewhere." She smiled at Lord Jennings, and Oliver felt as though someone had punched him hard in the stomach. "We had not yet fully decided."

"Then might I suggest both?" Lord Jennings said gallantly. "A walk to Berkley Square will not take us long, but I would be glad to accompany you both." He shot a quick look towards Oliver as though he had only just remembered he was there. "Do you wish to join us, Yarmouth?"

Not quite certain as to whether or not he would be welcomed, Oliver hesitated.

"You are most welcome to join us, Lord Yarmouth," Lady Croome said gently, finally holding his gaze as a gentle, forgiving smile settled across her face. "Please, do not hesitate on my account."

Oliver felt as though she had extended a hand of friendship towards him—a gesture he did not deserve. Not after all that he had said and done towards her. Lowering his head, he closed his eyes for a moment and then finally spoke.

"You are very gracious, Lady Croome," he said, thinking to himself that there was no other lady such as she in his acquaintance. "Thank you. I should be glad to join you."

Her smile grew, but her eyes immediately darted towards Lord Jennings, leaving Oliver caught between relief and confusion.

"Shall we depart?" Lady Croome asked, and, much to Oliver's astonishment, Lord Jennings stepped forward and offered Lady Croome his arm. With wide eyes, Oliver saw how she paused, looking up at Lord Jennings with a slightly confused glance before she accepted, allowing him to lead her away from Oliver and towards Gunter's.

"Are you going to stand there all afternoon, Lord Yarmouth?" Lady Ashbrook asked a few moments later. "Or do you intend to join us at Gunter's?"

Giving himself a slight shake, Oliver looked down

into the enquiring face of Lady Ashbrook. "Yes, of course," he managed, offering her his arm, which she took at once. "I must confess myself a little overcome at seeing Lady Croome again."

"And in seeing Lord Jennings' obvious attentions towards her, I should think," Lady Ashbrook said, a teasing note in her voice. "Although I am surprised that he has made such a hasty decision."

Oliver stopped dead, startling Lady Ashbrook, who stumbled slightly.

"What do you mean?" he asked, letting go of her arm as his heart began to pound furiously. "What do you mean about Lord Jennings?"

Lady Ashbrook let out a small huff and brushed down her skirts, evidently fearing that in her stumble, she had creased them. "Come now, Lord Yarmouth!" she said, a small frown etched across her brow. "Do not pretend that Lord Jennings has not spoken to you of this!"

"I can assure you he has not," Oliver replied, growing a little desperate to hear what it was that Lady Ashbrook knew. "He told me that he had thought of marrying and that his intention was to seek out a particular lady— someone he knew would be in town this afternoon, but I did not think that it would be..." He trailed off, seemingly unable to say Lady Croome's name.

Lady Ashbrook eyed him speculatively, then lifted one shoulder in a small shrug. "Mayhap he has not wanted to concern you with such things, given that there has been a small amount of difficulty between yourself and Lady Croome," she said in a matter of fact tone of voice. "But yes, it is as you think. Lady Croome is his intended lady, and he wrote to me earlier asking if I would be with her this afternoon so that he might meet us here in town. I am sure that it is simply a matter of deciding whether or not he truly wishes to settle his interest upon her, Lord Yarmouth, although I must say it does make a great deal of sense." Gesturing towards Lady Croome and Lord Jennings, she let out a small huff of exasperation. "We should at least attempt to keep alongside them, Lord Yarmouth."

She did not wait for him to respond but instead began to hurry after their friends. Oliver blinked rapidly, trying desperately to catch his breath as he struggled to comprehend all that Lady Ashbrook had said. Lord Jennings courting Lady Croome? It was, of course, quite understandable given that they were well acquainted with each other and knew the temperament and character of one another, but still, Oliver could not bring himself to be anywhere close to accepting it. Lady Croome could *not* wed Lord Jennings! It could not be permitted!

"Lord Yarmouth!" he heard Lady Ashbrook cry, her voice carrying towards him. "Do keep up!"

He could not move, could not even find the strength to answer her. Every muscle in his body trembled, his mind screamed at him, and still, he could not go after them both.

"Lord Yarmouth!" Lady Ashbrook had marched back towards him, her eyes fixed to his as she stood before him. "Have you taken ill?"

Swallowing hard, Oliver tried to nod, tried to say that yes, he was a little overcome, but instead could only close his eyes and make an indistinguishable noise in the back of his throat.

"I see," Lady Ashbrook said gently. "This news has astonished you, then."

Oliver opened his eyes. "Yes," he said hoarsely. "It has."

"And you need a little time to consider it," Lady Ashbrook continued with a gentle nod. "I quite understand. I shall tell Lady Croome and Lord Jennings that you thought to return home, perhaps wearied from the sun or some such excuse." She pressed his hand, her face holding a smile that he could not quite understand. "Return home, Lord Yarmouth. Think upon what has been told to you."

"I can hardly bear to," he rasped as Lady Ashbrook let go of his hand and looked up at him with sympathy glowing in her eyes. "This is all so unexpected, so...shocking."

"Then you must permit it to enter your heart and to, thereafter, decide what you shall do," Lady Ashbrook replied cryptically. "I am certain that you shall make the correct choice, Lord Yarmouth. Your heart is already aware of the answer. It is only for you to look therein and discover it." With another smile, she bobbed a quick curtsy and then turned away, making her way towards Gunter's and leaving Oliver standing alone on the pavement, not at all certain what he was supposed to do.

Permit it to enter your heart.

It was already there, he was sure of it. That was why his heart beat with such pain, with such agony. It was why the thought of Lord Jennings marrying Lady

Croome was so distasteful to him, why he could barely stand to even consider it.

A strange urge to rush to Gunter's, to pull Lord Jennings away and to demand to know precisely what he was doing, filled him, to the point of making him take a few steps forward—but Oliver stopped himself quickly. There was no reason that Lord Jennings could not court Lady Croome if she accepted it. So why then was he so afraid that she would accept Lord Jennings? He himself had no claim on her. There was nothing of significance between them; no promise or declaration that would bind him to her and her to him.

"But I want there to be," he murmured, finding himself utterly astonished as he spoke those words aloud. And, in that moment, it was as though the sun had decided to shine a little hotter, a little brighter and a little stronger upon him at that moment. The noise of those around him and the carriages upon the cobbled streets all faded away as finally, the truth of his heart hit him full force.

He cared for Lady Croome. Cared for her desperately, to the point that he could not think of her being wed to anyone.

"To anyone except for me," he breathed, his heart pounding furiously as he felt the realization of all that he sensed beginning to pour down within him, to reach out and grasp him tightly so that he could not do anything other than accept it.

This was astonishing. This was overwhelming. And this was completely and utterly wonderful.

Oliver did not quite know what to do next. Ought he

run to Gunther's, to declare himself before Lady Croome in the hope that she might feel the same? It would certainly be making a spectacle of himself, making certain that those about him knew precisely how he felt and, he realized, in doing so, he might bring a shame to Lady Croome also.

"Then it is not something I can do," he muttered to himself, a little deflated. Turning around, he began to make his way back towards his carriage, realizing that he would have to return home for the present. To throw himself at Lady Croome's feet would not be a wise decision given that she could react very badly indeed. Besides which, he recalled, his face burning in shame, he had treated her very poorly these last few days. It would surely throw her all the more into confusion if he simply appeared at Gunter's and told her what he had only just realized was within his heart!

"I must think on things a little longer," he murmured to himself, sitting back in his seat and rapping on the roof to instruct the driver to begin the short drive home. "And pray that, once I have the courage and the clarity of mind to speak to both Lord Jennings and Lady Croome, that I shall not be too late."

A sudden fear about what might occur should he *not* do so soon began to clamor at his mind, making him shudder violently. If he lingered for too long, then Lord Jennings might act promptly, might begin to court Lady Croome to the point that her attention would be fixed upon him rather than being open to what Oliver himself would have to say.

Closing his eyes, Oliver leaned back against the

squabs and tried to quieten his anxious thoughts. This was something he had to consider thoroughly and, thereafter, enact with great care. Lady Croome deserved the very best from him, and he was not about to let her down again. This time, every word he said would be well thought out, every single sentence measured and considered. He would lay out what he had come to learn about his own heart, would express to her all that he had done wrong and beg for her forgiveness. What she would say and what she would do thereafter, he could not begin to imagine. All he could do was hope.

CHAPTER FOURTEEN

Oliver drew in a long breath. Lord Jennings, Lady Croome, and Lord and Lady Ashbrook were all to join him this afternoon. It was drawing near to the time of their arrival, and Oliver had never once felt so anxious as he did at this moment. It was a very odd feeling, given that Lady Croome was one of his dearest friends and he had never felt such nervousness before when it came to being in her company. But this was the most important meeting of his acquaintance with the lady and one that simply had to go well. He could not afford to make any sort of mistake, had to speak with all the consideration that he could muster.

Blowing out a long breath, Oliver looked at himself in the mirror and ran one finger over his cravat, even though it was already perfect. He had taken the last two days to consider all that had been said to him by Lady Ashbrook and, thereafter, all that he had then come to realize about his own heart. It had been a great shock to realize that he had such a depth of affection for Lady Croome but, in looking back on his acquaintance with the ladies she had suggested for his wife, he understood now what he himself had been doing. Whether unconsciously or not, he had compared each one to Lady Croome, had felt them fall short in his estimation given that they did not meet the same standards as she did. To his mind, there was none better. Lady Marina's beauty had blinded him for a moment, had made him lose his senses, but Lady Croome's honest words had pulled the mask from his eyes and made him realize the truth.

His heart ached furiously as regret filled him. Had he only realized what he felt earlier, then he would have been able to speak to Lady Croome, might have spared them this strange set of circumstances which now took hold of them both. Knowing that he would, most likely, throw Lady Croome into an even *greater* confusion given what he was to say to her, Oliver closed his eyes and drew in a long breath. So long as he spoke carefully, then he could be certain that she would understand him without difficulty. All he could do was pray that she might be willing to, at the very least, consider him.

A scratch at the door made him jump, although he immediately cleared his throat and turned to face the door, calling for the butler to enter. Trying to place a welcoming smile on his face and pushing down his nervousness as best he could, Oliver placed his hands behind his back and prepared to meet his guests.

"Good evening, Lord Yarmouth," Lord Jennings exclaimed, walking into the room with Lady Croome on his arm as Lord and Lady Ashbrook came thereafter. They all greeted him warmly, and Oliver responded in kind, trying his utmost not to flinch at the sight of Lady Croome standing so close to Lord Jennings.

"Thank you all for coming," he said, grandly, gesturing to the refreshments that had been laid out. "You are all *most* welcome." He smiled warmly at each of them and allowed his gaze to linger on Lady Croome, who, he noted, blushed just a little as she glanced towards him.

Surely, that was a good sign.

"I thought we could just spend the evening conversing and enjoying each other's company," he said by way of explanation as they all took a seat in the drawing-room. "And Lady Ashbrook, might you play for us at some point this evening?"

"I should be glad to," Lady Ashbrook replied, smiling at him as her husband beamed with evident delight at his wife being so favored. "Should you like me to pour the tea for myself and Lady Croome?"

Oliver nodded, returning his gaze to Lady Croome. She was sitting demurely but, much to his displeasure, near to Lord Jennings, who was, Oliver noticed, smiling in a self-satisfied manner. At that moment, Oliver felt such a surge of dislike for his friend that it almost overpowered him, almost forced him to his feet, the words ready on his lips.

No.

Letting out a long breath slowly and carefully, Oliver reeled in his temper. He had told himself over and over that this evening was to be one of careful consideration and practiced words, but just seeing Lady Croome again threatened to shatter all of his intentions.

Thankfully, the conversation soon moved forward and Oliver found himself quietly able to calm himself without drawing the attention of others. Lady Croome seemed to be just as she normally was, evidently having set aside all of his poor conduct with a forgiveness he had not even asked her for.

How could I have been so blind?

"Perhaps I might play now?" Lady Ashbrook said, rising to her feet and making her way to the pianoforte. "Ashbrook, do come and turn the pages for me."

The moment was upon him sooner than he had expected, Oliver realized. Lady Ashbrook and Lord Ashbrook made their way to the pianoforte, and soon, gentle music began to fill the room. It was a quiet, sweet melody, but Oliver felt nothing but tension, looking to Lady Croome and Lord Jennings as they sat listening to the music.

He could wait no longer.

"Tell me, Jennings," he said abruptly, rising to his feet. "Do you intend to court Lady Croome?" His voice was sharper than he had intended, and no doubt there was a dark expression on his face, but Oliver could not remedy such a thing, try as he might. Lord Jennings blinked in surprise, speaking over the music as he replied.

"You have heard from Lady Ashbrook, it seems," he replied with a small shrug. "I have not asked the lady as yet, but I do have every intention of doing so." His eyes flicked to Lady Croome, who had gone a shade of pink. "That does not concern you, does it?"

"It does indeed," Oliver replied firmly. "I should have been glad to know of your intentions at the first, Jennings, for then I might have come to a particular realization sooner." Swallowing hard and feeling his stomach tie itself into tight knots, Oliver looked to Lady Croome. "I cannot allow Lord Jennings to speak to you in such a manner, Tabitha," he continued, aware of how she could barely look at him, her face now crimson.

"Allow me?" Lord Jennings repeated, sounding quite astonished. He, too, rose from his chair and then took a few steps closer to Oliver. "Whatever can you mean by that?"

Oliver turned to his friend. "We have long been friends, Jennings, but whatever intentions you might have for Lady Croome are nothing compared to what I have within my heart for her." His words were no longer the practiced speech that he had intended but spoken just as he felt them, giving way to all that he wanted to say without hesitation. Turning back to Lady Croome, he held out one hand to her. "If you will permit me, Tabitha, I should like to speak to you before Lord Jennings does so."

His heart was thumping furiously as he looked into Lady Croome's eyes, waiting to see whether or not she would accept him. If she did not, then his heart would be quite broken, whereas, if she did, then there was nothing that could compare with the amount of joy that he would feel.

Tentatively, Lady Croome reached out her hand and

took his, getting to her feet carefully. "But of course," she said, her eyes a little brighter than before. "Do excuse us, Lord Jennings."

"I quite understand," Lord Jennings replied, although, much to Oliver's confusion, the man was grinning inanely at Lady Croome as she made her way past him. What was he thinking? Did he believe that she would accept him regardless of what Oliver said?

Unable to wait for even a moment longer, Oliver hurried to the door and pulled it open, allowing Lady Croome to step out into the hallway. It was not the most private of spaces, but he could not linger any longer.

"Tabitha," he breathed, grasping her hands before she could take another step. "I am terribly sorry for all that I have done. I have spoken cruelly and foolishly and without consideration. I have found myself confused and frustrated and have not treated you with the respect and the consideration and the appreciation that you are due." His hands pressed hers. "For I *do* appreciate you, Tabitha. The thought of you retreating from my life has had me in agony. I cannot bear it. I..." Closing his eyes, he tried to bring to mind the words he had rehearsed but found that he could not do so. Nothing returned to him save for the awareness of just how much he cared for the lady before him. "I love you, Tabitha."

These last words were whispered and, as he looked down into her beautiful face, he felt his heart let out a sigh of relief. At the very least, he had been able to tell her the truth of how he felt even though it was still so new to him.

Lady Croome's eyes widened, and she caught her breath, her hands still tightly in his.

"I know it seems sudden," he said when she did not respond, "but I have only just become aware of it. I have spent these last weeks comparing the other ladies to you, finding that each does not match up to your wonderful character. Thinking of being separated from you—that Lord Jennings would be the one to marry you—was more than I could bear. I must ask you, Tabitha, if you would do me the honor of even *considering* marrying me, for it would be the greatest joy of my life."

Holding his breath, he pressed his lips together, afraid that he would say more instead of giving her the time to think about what he had said.

"Oliver," Lady Croome whispered, pulling her hands from his. In one awful moment, Oliver feared that she would step away from him, would refuse him, only for her hands to go about his neck as a brilliant, joyous smile spread across her face.

"Oh, Oliver, I have felt such a desperate longing these last few days that I have not known what to do!" she told him, making him laugh with astonishment. "Lady Ashbrook and Lord Jennings were quite convinced that you cared for me also and that the only way for you to realize it was to pretend that Lord Jennings had intentions towards me."

Oliver's mouth fell open. "You mean to say that it was nothing more than a ruse?"

"A ruse that brought about the response I had barely allowed myself to hope for," she replied, her face tilted towards his. "It was only a few days ago that I was shown the truth of my heart. Oh, Yarmouth, will you not marry me? Will you make me your bride? I swear that I shall bring you as much happiness as I can every day of my life."

Oliver swallowed her up in an embrace, his arms about her waist, his mouth finding hers as her fingers twined through his hair. It was a most astonishing and incredible moment, for he was kissing the one lady he had never considered kissing before, and yet it felt as though it was something he had always been dreaming of doing. His heart filled with all manner of emotion—happiness, delight, relief, exuberance—for there was no greater joy on this earth that finding his greatest hope fulfilled.

"I love you, Tabitha," he murmured as she pressed her forehead lightly to his, her eyes still closed. "Of course, we shall marry. I cannot think of anything I wish for more."

"Nor I," she replied, a contented sigh issuing from her lips. "For I love you in return, Yarmouth, and I know that from this day on, I shall always do so." Her eyes opened and fixed to his, her smile more beautiful than any he had ever seen before. "I am to be your wife," she whispered with such an expression of astonished delight that Oliver could not help but laugh with happiness. "And you my husband."

"And I your husband," he repeated before bending his head to kiss her once more.

. . .

I AM glad they came to their sense and realized their love for each other! I hope you enjoyed their story!

If you miss the first book in Convenient Arrangement series, give it a try! A Broken Betrothal

If you are caught up on that story, please try The Baron's Malady It is a lovely story centered around an epidemic!

MY DEAR READER

Thank you for reading and supporting my books! I hope this story brought you some escape from the real world into the always captivating Regency world. A good story, especially one with a happy ending, just brightens your day and makes you feel good! If you enjoyed the book, would you leave a review on Amazon? Reviews are always appreciated.

Below is a complete list of all my books! Why not click and see if one of them can keep you entertained for a few hours?

The Duke's Daughters Series
The Duke's Daughters: A Sweet Regency Romance
Boxset
A Rogue for a Lady
My Restless Earl
Rescued by an Earl
In the Arms of an Earl
The Reluctant Marquess (Prequel)

A Smithfield Market Regency Romance
The Smithfield Market Romances: A Sweet Regency
Romance Boxset
The Rogue's Flower

Saved by the Scoundrel
Mending the Duke
The Baron's Malady

The Returned Lords of Grosvenor Square
The Returned Lords of Grosvenor Square: A Regency
Romance Boxset
The Waiting Bride
The Long Return
The Duke's Saving Grace
A New Home for the Duke

The Spinsters Guild
A New Beginning
The Disgraced Bride
A Gentleman's Revenge
A Foolish Wager
A Lord Undone

Convenient Arrangements
A Broken Betrothal
In Search of Love
Wed in Disgrace
Betrayal and Lies
A Past to Forget
Engaged to a Friend

Christmas Stories
Love and Christmas Wishes: Three Regency Romance
Novellas
A Family for Christmas

Mistletoe Magic: A Regency Romance
Home for Christmas Series Page

Happy Reading!

All my love,

Rose

A SNEAK PEAK OF A BROKEN BETROTHAL

PROLOGUE

L ady Augusta looked at her reflection in the mirror and sighed inwardly. She had tried on almost every gown in her wardrobe and still was not at all decided on which one she ought to wear tonight. She had to make the right decision, given that this evening was to be her first outing into society since she had returned to London.

"Augusta, what in heaven's name...?" The sound of her mother's voice fading away as she looked all about the room and saw various gowns strewn everywhere, the maids quickening to stand straight, their heads bowed as the countess came into the room. Along with her came a friend of Lady Elmsworth, whom Augusta knew very well indeed, although it was rather embarrassing to have her step into the bedchamber when it was in such a disarray!

"Good afternoon, Mama," Augusta said, dropping into a quick curtsy. "And good afternoon, Lady Newfield." She took in Lady Newfield's face, seeing the twinkle in the lady's blue eyes and the way her lips twitched, which was in direct contrast to her mother, who was standing with her hands on her hips, clearly upset.

"Would you like to explain, my dear girl, what it is that you are doing here?" The countess looked into Augusta's face, her familiar dark eyes sharpening. Augusta tried to smile but her mother only narrowed her eyes and planted her hands on her hips, making it quite plain that she was greatly displeased with what Augusta was doing.

"Mama," Augusta wheedled, gesturing to her gowns. "You know that I must look my very best for this evening's ball. "Therefore, I must be certain that I—"

"We had already selected a gown, Augusta," Lady Elmsworth interrupted, quieting Augusta's excuses immediately. "You and I went to the dressmaker's only last week and purchased a few gowns that would be worn for this little Season. The first gown you were to wear was, if I recall, that primrose yellow." She indicated a gown that was draped over Augusta's bed, and Augusta felt heat rise into her face as the maids scurried to pick it up.

"I do not think it suits my coloring, Mama," she said, a little half-heartedly. "You are correct to state that we chose it together, but I have since reconsidered."

Lady Newfield cleared her throat, with Lady Elmsworth darting a quick look towards her.

"I would be inclined to agree, Lady Elmsworth," she said, only for Lady Elmsworth to throw up one hand, bringing her friend's words to a swift end. Augusta's hopes died away as her mother's thin brows began knitting together with displeasure. "That is enough, Augusta," she said firmly, ignoring Lady Newfield entirely. "That gown will do you very well, just as we discussed." She looked at the maids. "Tidy the rest of these up at once and ensure that the primrose yellow is left for this evening."

The maids curtsied and immediately set to their task, leaving Augusta to merely sit and watch as the maids obeyed the mistress of the house rather than doing what she wanted. In truth, the gown that had been chosen for her had been mostly her mother's choice, whilst she had attempted to make gentle protests that had mostly been ignored. With her dark brown hair and green eyes, Augusta was sure that the gown did, in fact, suit her coloring very well, but she did not want to be clad in yellow, not when so many other debutantes would be wearing the same. No, Augusta wanted to stand out, to be set apart, to be noticed! She had come to London only a few months ago for the Season and had been delighted when her father had encouraged them to return for the little Season. Thus, she had every expectation of finding a suitable husband and making a good match. However, given how particular her mother was being over her gown, Augusta began to worry that her mother would soon begin to choose Augusta's dance partners and the like so that she would have no independence whatsoever!

"I think I shall return to our tea," Lady Newfield said gently as Lady Elmsworth gave her friend a jerky nod. "I apologize for the intrusion, Lady Augusta."

"There was no intrusion," Augusta said quickly, seeing the small smile that ran around Lady Newfield's mouth and wishing that her mother had been a little more willing to listen to her friend's comments. For what-ever reason, she felt as though Lady Newfield understood her reasoning more than her mother did.

"Now, Augusta," Lady Elmsworth said firmly, settling herself in a chair near to the hearth where a fire burned brightly, chasing away the chill of a damp winter afternoon. "This evening, you are to be introduced to one gentleman in particular. I want you to ensure that you behave impeccably. Greet him warmly and correctly, but thereafter, do not say a good deal."

Augusta frowned, her eyes searching her mother's face for answers that Lady Elmsworth was clearly unwilling to give. "Might I ask why I am to do such a thing, Mama?"

Lady Elmsworth held Augusta's gaze for a moment, and then let out a small sigh. "You will be displeased, of course, for you are always an ungrateful sort but none-theless, you ought to find some contentment in this." She waited a moment as though waiting to see if Augusta had some retort prepared already, only to shrug and then continue. "Your father has found you a suitable match, Augusta. You are to meet him this evening."

The world seemed to stop completely as Augusta stared at her mother in horror. The footsteps of the maids came to silence; the quiet crackling of the fire turned to naught. Her chest heaved with great breaths as Augusta tried to accept what she had just been told, closing her eyes to shut out the view of her mother's slightly bored expression. This was not what she had expected. Coming back to London had been a matter of great excitement for her, having been told that *this* year would be the year for her to make a suitable match. She had never once thought that such a thing would be pulled from her, removed from her grasp entirely. Her father had never once mentioned that he would be doing such a thing but now, it seemed, he had chosen to do so without saying a word to her about his intentions.

"Do try to form some response, Augusta," Lady Elmsworth said tiredly. "I am aware this is something of a surprise, but it is for your own good. The gentleman in question has an excellent title and is quite wealthy." She waved a hand in front of her face as though such things were the only things in the world that mattered. "It is not as though you could have found someone on your own, Augusta."

"I should have liked the opportunity to try," Augusta whispered, hardly able to form the words she wanted so desperately to say.

"You had the summer Season," Lady Elmsworth retorted with a shrug. "Do you not recall?"

Augusta closed her eyes. The summer Season had been her first outing into society, and she had enjoyed every moment of it. Her father and mother had made it quite plain that this was not to be the year where she found a husband but rather a time for her to enjoy society, to become used to what it meant to live as a member of the *ton*. The little Season and the summer Season thereafter, she had been told, would be the ones for her to seek out a husband.

And now, that had been pulled away from her before she had even had the opportunity to be amongst the gentlemen of the *beau monde*.

"As I have said," Lady Elmsworth continued, briskly, ignoring Augusta's complaint and the clear expression of shock on her face, "there is no need for you to do anything other than dress in the gown we chose together and then to ensure that you greet Lord Pendleton with all refinement and propriety."

Augusta closed her eyes. "Lord Pendleton?" she repeated, tremulously, already afraid that this gentleman was some older, wealthy gentleman who, for whatever reason, had not been able to find a wife and thus had been more than eager to accept her father's offer.

"Did I not say?" Lady Elmsworth replied, sounding somewhat distracted. She rose quickly, her skirts swishing noisily as she walked towards the door. "He is brother to the Marquess of Leicestershire. A fine gentleman, by all accounts." She shrugged. "He is quiet and perhaps a little dull, but he will do very well for you." One of the maids held the door open, and before Augusta could say more, her mother swept out of the room and the door was closed tightly behind her.

Augusta waited for tears to come but they did not even begin to make their way towards her eyes. She was numb all over, cold and afraid of what was to come. This was not something she had even considered a possibility when it came to her own considerations for what the little Season would hold. There had always been the belief that she would be able to dance, converse, and laugh with as many gentlemen as thought to seek her out. In time, there would be courtships and one gentleman in particular might bring themselves to her notice. There would be excitement and anticipation, nights spent reading and re-reading notes and letters from the gentleman in question, her heart quickening at the thought of marrying him.

But now, such thoughts were gone from her. There was to be none of what she had expected, what she had hoped for. Instead, there was to be a meeting and an arrangement, with no passion or excitement.

Augusta closed her eyes and finally felt a sting of tears. Dropping her head into her hands, she let her emotions roar to life, sending waves of feeling crashing through her until, finally, Augusta wept.

CHAPTER ONE

Q uite why he had arranged to be present this evening, Stephen did not know. He ought to have stated that he would meet Lady Augusta in a quieter setting than a ball so that he might have talked with her at length rather than forcing a quick meeting upon them both in a room where it was difficult to hear one's own voice such was the hubbub of the crowd.

He sighed and looked all about him again, finding no delight in being in the midst of society once more. He was a somewhat retiring gentleman, finding no pleasure in the gossip and rumors that flung themselves all around London during the little Season, although it was always much worse during the summer Season. Nor did he appreciate the falseness of those who came to speak and converse with him, knowing full well that the only reason they did so was to enquire after his brother, the Marquess of Leicestershire.

His brother was quite the opposite in both looks and

character, for where Stephen had light brown hair with blue eyes, his brother had almost black hair with dark brown eyes that seemed to pierce into the very soul of whomever he was speaking with. The ladies of the *ton* wanted nothing more than to be in the presence of Lord Leicestershire and, given he was absent from society, they therefore came towards Stephen in order to find out what they could about his brother.

It was all quite wearisome, and Stephen did not enjoy even a moment of it. He was not as important as his brother, he knew, given he did not hold the high title nor have the same amount of wealth as Lord Leicestershire, but surely his own self, his conversation and the like, was of *some* interest? He grinned wryly to himself as he picked up a glass from the tray held by a footman, wondering silently to himself that, if he began to behave as his brother had done on so many occasions, whether or not that would garner him a little more interest from rest of the *ton*.

"You look much too contented," said a familiar voice, and Stephen looked to his left to see his acquaintance, Lord Dryden, approach him. Lord Dryden, a viscount, had an estate near the border to Scotland and, whilst lower in title than Stephen, had become something of a close acquaintance these last two years.

"Lord Dryden," Stephen grinned, slapping the gentleman on the back. "How very good to see you again."

Lord Dryden chuckled. "And you," he said with an honest look in his eyes. "Now, tell me why you are standing here smiling to yourself when I know very well that a ball is not the sort of event you wish to attend?"

Stephen's grin remained on his lips, his eyes alighting on various young ladies that swirled around him. "I was merely considering what my life might be like if I chose to live as my brother does," he answered, with a shrug. "I should have all of society chasing after me, I suppose, although a good many would turn their heads away from me with the shame of being in my company."

"That is quite true," Lord Dryden agreed, no smile on his face but rather a look of concern. "You do not wish to behave so, I hope?"

"No, indeed, I do not," Stephen answered firmly, his smile fading away. "I confess that I am growing weary of so many in the *ton* coming to seek me out simply because they wish to know more about my brother."

"He is not present this evening?"

Stephen snorted. "He is not present for the little Season," he replied with a shrug of his shoulders. "Do not ask me what he has been doing, or why he has such a notable absence, for I fear I cannot tell you." Setting his shoulders, he let out a long breath. "No, I must look to my future."

"Indeed," Lord Dryden responded, an interested look on his face as he eyed Stephen speculatively. "And what is it about your future that you now consider?"

Stephen cleared his throat, wondering whether he ought to tell his friend even though such an arrangement had not yet been completely finalized. "I am to consider myself betrothed very soon," he said before he lost his nerve and kept such news to himself. "I am to meet the lady here this evening. Her father has already signed the papers and they await me in my study." He shrugged one shoulder. "I am sure that, provided she has not lost all of her teeth and that her voice is pleasant enough, the betrothal will go ahead as intended."

Lord Dryden stared at Stephen for a few moments, visible shock rippling over his features. His eyes were wide and his jaw slack, without even a single flicker of mirth in his gaze as he looked back at him. Stephen felt his stomach drop, now worried that Lord Dryden would make some remark that would then force Stephen to reconsider all that he had decided thus far, fearful now that he had made some foolish mistake.

"Good gracious!" Lord Dryden began to laugh, his hand grasping Stephen's shoulder tightly. "You are betrothed?" Shaking his head, he let out another wheezing laugh before straightening and looking Stephen directly in the eye. "I should have expected such a thing from you, I suppose, given you are always entirely practical and very well-considered, but I had not expected it so soon!"

"So soon?" Stephen retorted with a chuckle. "I have been in London for the last three Seasons and have found not even a single young lady to be interested in even conversing with me without needing to talk solely about my brother." His lip curled, a heaviness sitting back on his shoulders as he let out a long sigh. "Therefore, this seemed to be the wisest and the most practical of agreements."

Lord Dryden chuckled again, his eyes still filled with good humor. "I am glad to hear it," he said warmly. "I do congratulate you, of course! Pray, forgive me for my humor. It is only that it has come as something of a surprise to hear such a thing from you yet, now that I consider it, it makes a good deal of sense!" He chuckled again and the sound began to grate on Stephen, making him frown as he returned his friend's sharp look.

Lord Dryden did not appear to care, even if he did notice Stephen's ire. Instead, he leaned a little closer, his eyes bright with curiosity. "Pray, tell me," he began as Stephen nodded, resigning himself to a good many questions. "Who is this lady? Is she of good quality?"

"Very good, yes," Stephen replied, aware, while he did not know the lady's features or character, that she came from a good family line and that breeding would not be a cause for concern. "She is Lady Augusta, daughter to the Earl of Elmsworth."

Lord Dryden's eyes widened, and his smile faded for a moment. "Goodness," he said quietly, looking at Stephen as though he feared his friend had made some sort of dreadful mistake. "And you have met the lady in question?"

"I am to meet her this evening," Stephen answered quickly, wondering why Lord Dryden now appeared so surprised. "I have not heard anything disreputable about her, however." He narrowed his gaze and looked at his friend sharply. "Why? Have you heard some rumor I have not?"

Lord Dryden held up both his hands in a gesture of defense. "No, indeed not!" he exclaimed, sounding quite horrified. "No, tis only that she is a lady who is very well thought of in society. She is well known to everyone, seeks to converse with them all, and has a good many admirers." One shoulder lifted in a half shrug. "To know that her father has sought out an arrangement for her surprises me a little, that is all."

"Because she could do very well without requiring an arrangement," Stephen said slowly understanding what Lord Dryden meant. "Her father appeared to be quite eager to arrange such a thing, however." He sighed and looked all about him, wondering when Lord Elmsworth and his daughter would appear. "He and I spoke at Whites when the matter of his daughter came up."

"And the arrangement came from there?" Lord Dryden asked as Stephen nodded. "I see." He lapsed into silence for a moment, then nodded as though satisfied that he had asked all the questions he wished. "Very good. Then may I be the first to congratulate you!" Lord Dryden's smile returned, and he held out a hand for Stephen to shake. Stephen did so after only a momentary hesitation, reminding himself that there was not, as yet, a complete agreement between himself and Lord Elmsworth.

"I still have to sign and return the papers," he reminded Lord Dryden, who made a noise in the back of his throat before shrugging. "You do not think there will be any difficulty there, I presume?"

"Of course there will not be any difficulty," Lord Dryden retorted with a roll of his eyes. "Lady Augusta is very pleasing, indeed. I am sure you will have no particular difficulty with her."

Stephen opened his mouth to respond, only to see someone begin to approach him. His heart quickened in his chest as he looked at them a little more carefully, seeing Lord Elmsworth approaching and, with him, a young lady wearing a primrose yellow gown. She had an elegant and slender figure and was walking in a most demure fashion, with eyes that lingered somewhere near his knees rather than looking up into people's faces. Her dark brown hair was pulled away from her face, with one or two small ringlets tumbling down near her temples, so as to soften the severity of it. When she dared a glance at him, he was certain he caught a hint of emerald green in her eyes. Almost immediately, her gaze returned to the floor as she dropped into a curtsy, Lord Elmsworth only a step or two in front of her.

"Lord Pendleton!" Lord Elmsworth exclaimed, shaking Stephen's hand with great enthusiasm. "Might I present my daughter, Lady Augusta." He beamed at his daughter, who was only just rising from what had been a perfect curtsy.

"Good evening, Lady Augusta," Stephen said, bowing before her. "I presume your father has already made quite plain who I am?" He looked keenly into her face, and when she lifted her eyes to his, he felt something strike at his heart.

It was not warmth, however, nor a joy that she was quietly beautiful. It did not chime with happiness or contentment but rather with a warning. A warning that Lady Augusta was not as pleased with this arrangement as he. A warning that he might come to trouble if he continued as had been decided. She was looking at him with a hardness in her gaze that hit him hard. There was a coldness, a reserve in her expression, that he could not escape. Clearly, Lady Augusta was not at all contented with the arrangement her father had made for her, which, in turn, did not bode well for him.

"Yes," Lady Augusta said after a moment or two, her voice just as icy as her expression. "Yes, my father has informed of who you are, Lord Pendleton." She looked away, her chin lifted, clearly finding there to be no desire otherwise to say anything more.

Stephen cleared his throat, glancing towards Lord Dryden, who was, to his surprise, not watching Lady Augusta as he had expected, but rather had his attention focused solely on Lord Elmsworth. There was a dark frown on his face; his eyes narrowed just a little and a clear dislike began to ripple across his expression. What was it that Lord Dryden could see that Stephen himself could not?

"Might I introduce Viscount Dryden?" he said quickly, before he could fail in his duties. "Viscount Dryden, this is the Earl of Elmsworth and his daughter—"

"We are already acquainted," Lord Dryden interrupted, bowing low before lifting his head, looking nowhere but at Lady Augusta. "It is very pleasant to see you again, Lady Augusta. I hope you are enjoying the start of the little Season."

Something in her expression softened, and Stephen saw Lady Augusta's mouth curve into a gentle smile. She answered Lord Dryden politely and Stephen soon found himself growing a little embarrassed at the easy flow of conversation between his friend and his betrothed. There was not that ease of manner within himself, he realized, dropping his head just a little so as to regain his sense of composure.

"Perhaps I might excuse myself for a short time," Lord Elmsworth interrupted before Lord Dryden could ask Lady Augusta another question. "Lady Elmsworth is standing but a short distance away and will be watching my daughter closely."

Stephen glanced to his right and saw an older lady looking directly at him, her sense of haughtiness rushing towards him like a gust of wind. There was no contentment in her eyes, but equally, there was no dislike either. Rather, there was the simple expectation that this was how things were to be done and that they ought to continue without delay.

"But of course, Lord Elmsworth," Stephen said quickly, bowing slightly. "I should like to sign your daughter's dance card, if I may?"

"I think," came Lady Augusta's voice, sharp and brittle, "then if that is the case, you ought to be asking the lady herself whether or not she has any space remaining on her card for you to do such a thing, Lord Pendleton."

There came an immediate flush of embarrassment onto Stephen's face, and he cleared his throat whilst Lord Elmsworth sent a hard glance towards his daughter, which she ignored completely. Only Lord Dryden chuckled, the sound breaking the tension and shattering it into a thousand pieces as Stephen looked away.

"You are quite correct to state such a thing, Lady Augusta," Lord Dryden said, easily. "You must forgive my friend. I believe he was a little apprehensive about this meeting and perhaps has forgotten quite how things are done."

Stephen's smile was taut, but he forced it to his lips regardless. "But of course, Lady Augusta," he said tightly. "Might you inform me whether or not you have any spaces on your dance card that I might then be able to take from you?" He bowed his head and waited for her to respond, seeing Lord Elmsworth move away from them all without waiting to see what his daughter would say.

"I thank you for your kind consideration in requesting such a thing from me," Lady Augusta answered, a little too saucily for his liking. "Yes, I believe I do have a few spaces, Lord Pendleton. Please, choose whichever you like." She handed him her dance card and then pulled her hand back, the ribbon sliding from her wrist as he looked down at it. She turned her head away as if she did not want to see where he wrote his name, and this, in itself, sent a flurry of anger down Stephen's spine. What was wrong with this young lady? Was she not glad that she was now betrothed, that she would soon have a husband and become mistress of his estate?

For a moment, he wondered if he had made a mistake in agreeing to this betrothal, feeling a swell of relief in his chest that he had not yet signed the agreement, only for Lord Dryden to give him a tiny nudge, making him realize he had not yet written his name down on the dance card but was, in fact, simply staring at it as though it might provide him with all the answers he required.

"The country dance, mayhap," he said, a little more loudly than he had intended. "Would that satisfy you, Lady Augusta?"

She turned her head and gave him a cool look, no smile gracing her lips. "But of course," she said with more sweetness than he had expected. "I would be glad to dance with you, Lord Pendleton. The country dance sounds quite wonderful."

He frowned, holding her gaze for a moment longer before dropping his eyes back to her dance card again and writing his name there. Handing it back to her, he waited for her to smile, to acknowledge what he had given her, only for her to sniff, bob a curtsy and turn away. Stephen's jaw worked furiously, but he remained standing steadfastly watching after her, refusing to allow himself to chase after her and demand to know what she meant by such behavior. Instead, he kept his head lifted and his eyes fixed, thinking to himself that he had, most likely, made a mistake.

"I would ascertain from her behavior that this betrothal has come as something of a shock," Lord Dryden murmured, coming closer to Stephen and looking after Lady Augusta with interest. "She was less than pleased to be introduced to you, that is for certain!"

Stephen blew out his frustration in a long breath, turning his eyes away from Lady Augusta and looking at his friend. "I think I have made a mistake," he said gruffly. "That young lady will not do at all! She is—"

"She is overcome," Lord Dryden interrupted, holding up one hand to stem the protest from Stephen's lips. "As I have said, I think this has been something of a shock to her. You may recall that I said I am acquainted with Lady Augusta already and I know that how she presented herself this evening is not her usual character."

Stephen shook his head, his lips twisting as he considered what he was to do. "I am not certain that I have made the wisest decision," he said softly. "Obviously, I require a wife and that does mean that I shall have to select someone from amongst the *ton,* but—"

"Lady Augusta is quite suitable," Lord Dryden interrupted firmly. "And, if you were quite honest with yourself, Lord Pendleton, I think you would find that such an arrangement suits you very well. After all—" He gestured to the other guests around him. "You are not at all inclined to go out amongst the *ton* and find a lady of your choosing, are you?"

Stephen sighed heavily and shot Lord Dryden a wry look. "That is true enough, I suppose."

"Then trust me when I say that Lady Augusta is more than suitable for you," Lord Dryden said again, with such fervor that Stephen felt as though he had no other choice to believe him. "Sign the betrothal agreement and know that Lady Augusta will not be as cold towards you in your marriage as she has been this evening." He chuckled and slapped Stephen on the shoulder. "May I be the first to offer you my congratulations."

Smiling a little wryly, Stephen found himself nodding. "Very well," he told Lord Dryden. "I accept your congratulations with every intention of signing the betrothal agreement when I return home this evening."

"Capital!" Lord Dryden boomed, looking quite satisfied with himself. "Then I look forward to attending your wedding in the knowledge that it was I who brought it about." He chuckled and then, spotting a young lady coming towards him quickly excused himself. Stephen smiled as he saw Lord Dryden offer his arm to the young lady and then step out on to the floor. His friend was correct. Lady Augusta was, perhaps, a little overwhelmed with all that had occurred and simply was not yet open to the fact that she would soon be his wife. In time, she would come to be quite happy with him and their life together; he was sure of it. He had to thrust his worries aside and accept his decisions for what they were.

"I shall sign it the moment I return home," he said aloud to himself as though confirming this was precisely what he intended to do. With a small sigh of relief at his decision, he lifted his chin and set his shoulders. Within the week, everyone would know of his betrothal to Lady Augusta and that, he decided, brought him a good deal of satisfaction.

HIS QUILL HOVERED over the line for just a moment but, with a clenching of his jaw, Stephen signed his name on the agreement. His breath shot out of him with great fury, leaving him swallowing hard, realizing what he had done. It was now finalized. He would marry Lady Augusta, and the banns would have to be called very soon, given her father wanted her wed before the end of the little Season. Letting out his breath slowly, he rolled up the papers and began to prepare his seal, only for there to come a hurried knock at the door. He did not even manage to call out for his servant to enter, for the butler rushed in before he could open his mouth.

"Do forgive me, my lord," the butler exclaimed, breathing hard from his clear eagerness to reach Stephen in time. "This came from your brother's estate with a most urgent request that you read it at once."

Startled, his stomach twisting one way and then the other, Stephen took the note from the butler's hand and opened it, noting that there was no print on the seal. His heart began to pound as he read the news held within.

"My brother is dead," he whispered, one hand gripping onto the edge of his desk for support. "He...he was shot in a duel and died on the field." Closing his eyes, Stephen let the news wash over him, feeling all manner of strong emotions as he fought to understand what had occurred. His brother had passed away, then, lost to the grave, and out of nothing more than his foolishness. To have been fighting in a duel meant that Leicestershire had done something of the most grievous nature—whether it had been stealing another man's wife or taking affections from some unfortunate young lady without any intention of pursuing the matter further.

Running one hand over his face, Stephen felt the weight of his grief come to settle on his heart, his whole body seeming to ache with a pain he had only experienced once before when their dear father had passed away. His throat constricted as he thought of his mother. He would have to go to her at once, to comfort her in the midst of her sorrow. Yes, his brother had packed her off to the Dower House long before she was due to reside there, and yes, there had been some difficulties between them, but Stephen knew that she had loved her eldest son and would mourn the loss of him greatly.

A groan came from his lips as he lifted his head and tried to focus on his butler. His vision was blurry, his head feeling heavy and painful.

"Ready my carriage at once," he rasped, "and have my things sent after me. I must return to my brother's estate."

The butler bowed. "At once," he said, his concern clear in his wide-eyed expression. "I beg your pardon for my intrusion, my lord, but is Lord Leicestershire quite well?"

Stephen looked at his faithful butler, knowing that the man had worked for the family for many years in keeping the townhouse in London readied for them and understood that his concern was genuine. "My brother is dead," he said hoarsely as the butler gasped in horror. "I have lost him. He is gone, and I shall never see him again."

CHAPTER TWO

S*ix months later*

AUGUSTA ROLLED her eyes as her mother brought out
the primrose yellow dress that she had worn at the start of
the little Season some six months ago. She sighed as her
mother spread it out with one hand, a look in her eye that
told Augusta she was not about to escape this easily.

"That gown was for the winter, Mama," she said,
calmly. "I cannot wear it again now that the sun is
shining and the air is so very warm." She gestured to it
with a look of what she hoped was sadness on her face.
"Besides, it is not quite up to the fashion for this current
Season."

Her mother tutted. "Nonsense, Augusta," she said
briskly. "There is very little need for you to purchase new
gowns when you are to have a trousseau. Your betrothed
has, as you know, recently lost his brother and as such,

will need to find some happiness in all that he does. I must hope that your presence will bring him a little joy in his sorrow and, in wearing the very same gown as you were first introduced to him in, I am certain that Lord Pendleton—I mean, Lord Leicestershire—will be very happy to see you again."

Augusta said nothing, silently disagreeing with her mother and having no desire whatsoever to greet her betrothed again, whether in her primrose yellow gown or another gown entirely. She had felt compassion and sympathy for his loss, yes, but she had silently reveled in her newfound freedom. Indeed, given their betrothal had not yet been confirmed and given the *ton* knew nothing of it, Augusta had spent the rest of the little Season enjoying herself, silently ignoring the knowledge that within the next few months, she would have to let everyone in the *ton* know of her engagement.

But not yet, it seemed. She had spoken to her father, and he had confirmed that the papers had not been returned by Lord Leicestershire but had urged her not to lose hope, stating that he had every reason to expect the gentleman to do just as he had promised but that he was permitting him to have some time to work through his grief before pressing him about the arrangement.

And when news had been brought that the new Marquess of Leicestershire had come to London for the Season, her father had taken it as confirmation that all was just as it ought to be. He was quite contented with the situation as things stood, silently certain that when Lord Leicestershire was ready, he would approach the Earl himself or speak directly to Augusta.

"I will not wear that gown, Mama," Augusta said frostily. "I am well aware of what you hope for but I cannot agree. That gown is not at all suitable for Lord Stonington's ball! I must find something that is quite beautiful, Mama." She saw her mother frown and tried quickly to come up with some reason for her to agree to such a change. "I know your intentions are good," she continued, swiftly, "but Lord Leicestershire will be glad to see me again no matter what I am wearing; I am sure of it. And, Mama, if I wear the primrose yellow gown, might it not remind him of the night that he was told of his brother's death?" She let her voice drop low, her eyes lowering dramatically. "The night when he had no other choice but to run from London so that he might comfort his mother and tidy up the ruin his brother left behind."

"Augusta!" Lady Elmsworth's voice was sharp. "Do not speak in such a callous manner!"

Augusta, who was nothing if not practical, looked at her mother askance. "I do not consider speaking the truth plainly to be callous, Mama," she said quite calmly. "After all, it is not as though Lord Leicestershire's brother was anything other than a scoundrel." She shrugged, turning away from her mother and ignoring the horrified look on her face. "Everyone in London is well aware what occurred."

She herself had been unable to escape the gossip and, to her shame, had listened to it eagerly at times. The late Lord Leicestershire had lost his life in a duel that had not gone well for him. He had taken a young lady of quality and attempted to steal kisses—and perhaps more—from her, only to be discovered by the young lady's brother, who was a viscount of some description. Despite the fact that such duels were frowned upon, one had taken place and the gentleman who had done such a dreadful thing to a young lady of society had paid the ultimate price for his actions. A part of her did feel very sorry indeed for the newly titled Lord Leicestershire, knowing that he must have had to endure a good deal of struggle, difficulty and pain in realizing not only what his brother had done but in taking on all the responsibilities that now came with his new title.

"I should think you better than to listen to gossip," Lady Elmsworth said, primly. "Now, Augusta, do stop being difficult and wear what I ask of you."

"No," Augusta replied quite firmly, surprising both herself and her mother with her vehemence. "No, I shall not." Taking in the look of astonishment on her mother's face, Augusta felt her spirits lift very high indeed as she realized that, if she spoke with determination, her mother might, in fact, allow her to do as she wished. She had, thus far, always bowed to her mother's authority, but ever since she had discovered that her marriage was already planned for her and that she was to have no independence whatsoever, she had found a small spark growing steadily within her. A spark that determined that she find some way to have a little autonomy, even if it would only be for a short time.

"I will wear the light green silk," she said decisively, walking to her wardrobe and indicating which one she meant. "It brings out my complexion a little more, I think." She smiled to herself and touched the fabric gently. "And I believe it brings a little more attention to my eyes."

Lady Elmsworth sighed heavily but, thankfully, she set down the primrose yellow and then proceeded to seat herself in a chair by the fire, which was not lit today given the warmth of the afternoon. "You think this is the most suitable choice, then?"

"I do," Augusta said firmly. "I shall wear this and have a few pearls and perhaps a ribbon set into my hair." Again, she smiled but did not see her mother's dark frown. "And perhaps that beautiful diamond pendant around my neck."

Lady Elmsworth's frown deepened. "You need not try to draw attention to yourself, Augusta," she reminded her sternly. "You are betrothed. You will be wed to Lord Leicestershire and he is the only one you need attempt to impress."

Augusta hid the sigh from her mother as she turned back to her wardrobe, closing the door carefully so as not to crush any of her gowns. A part of her hoped that she would not have to marry Lord Leicestershire, for given he had not yet returned the betrothal agreement to her father, there seemed to be no eagerness on his part to do so or to proceed with their engagement. Mayhap, now that he was of a great and high title, he might find himself a little more interested in the young ladies of the *ton* and would not feel the need to sign the betrothal agreement at all. It might all come to a very satisfactory close, and she could have the freedom she had always expected.

"Augusta!" Lady Elmsworth's voice was sharp, as though she knew precisely what it was Augusta was thinking. "You will make sure that all of your attention is on your betrothed this evening. Do you understand me?"

"We are not betrothed yet, Mama," Augusta replied a little tartly. "Therefore, I cannot show him any specific attention for fear of what others might say." She arched one eyebrow and looked at her mother as she turned around, aware she was irritating her parent but finding a dull sense of satisfaction in her chest. "Once the agreement has been sent to Papa, then, of course, I shall do my duty." She dropped into a quick curtsy, her eyes low and her expression demure, but it did not fool Lady Elmsworth.

"You had best be very careful with your behavior this evening, Augusta," she exclaimed, practically throwing herself from her chair as she rose to her feet, her cheeks a little pink and her eyes blazing with an unexpressed frustration. "I shall be watching you most carefully."

"Of course, Mama," Augusta replied quietly, permitting herself a small smile as her mother left the room, clearly more than a little irritated with all that Augusta had said. Augusta let a long breath escape her, feeling a sense of anticipation and anxiety swirl all about within her as she considered what was to come this evening. Lord Leicestershire would be present, she knew, for whilst he had not written to her directly to say such a thing, all of London was abuzz with the news that the new Marquess had sent his acceptance to Lord Stonington's ball. Everyone would want to look at him, to see his face and to wonder just how like his brother he might prove to be. Everyone, of course, except for Augusta. She would greet him politely, of course, but had no intention of showing any interest in him whatsoever. Perhaps that, combined with his new title and his new appreciation from the *ton,* might decide that she was no longer a suitable choice for a wife.

Augusta could only hope.

"Good evening, Lady Augusta."

Augusta gasped in surprise as she turned to see who had spoken her name, before throwing herself into the arms of a lovely lady. "Lady Mary!" she cried, delighted to see her dear friend again. They had shared one Season already as debutantes and had become very dear friends indeed, and Augusta had missed her at the little Season. "How very glad I am to see you again. I am in desperate need of company and you have presented yourself to me at the very moment that I need you!"

Lady Mary laughed and squeezed Augusta's hand. "But of course," she said, a twinkle in her eye. "I knew very well that you would need a dear friend to walk through this Season with you—just as I need one also!" She turned and looked at the room, the swirling colors of the gowns moving all around them, and let out a contented sigh. "I am quite certain that this Season, we shall both find a suitable match, and I, for one, am eagerly looking forward to the courtship, the excitement and the wonderfulness that is sure to follow!"

Augusta could not join in with the delight that Lady Mary expressed, her heart suddenly heavy and weighted as it dropped in her chest. Lady Mary noticed at once, her joyous smile fading as she looked into Augusta's face.

"My dear friend, whatever is the matter?"

Augusta opened her mouth to answer, only for her gaze to snag on something. Or, rather, a familiar face that seemed to loom out of the crowd towards her, her heart slamming hard as she realized who it was.

"Lady Augusta?"

Lady Mary's voice seemed to be coming from very far away as Augusta's eyes fixed upon Lord Leicestershire, her throat constricting and a sudden pain stabbing into her chest. He was standing a short distance away, and even though there were other guests coming in and out of her vision, blocking her view of him entirely upon occasion, she seemed to be able to see him quite clearly. His eyes were fixed to hers, appearing narrowed and dark and filled with nothing akin to either gladness or relief upon seeing her. Her stomach dropped to the floor for an inexplicable reason, making her wonder if he felt the same about her as she did about him. Why did that trouble her, she wondered, unable to tug her gaze from his. She should be able to turn her head away from him at once, should be able to show the same disregard as she had done at their first meeting, should be able to express her same dislike for their arrangement as she had done at the first—but for whatever reason, she was not able to do it.

"Lady Augusta, you are troubling me now!"

Lady Mary's voice slowly came back to her ears, growing steadily louder until the hubbub of the room appeared to be much louder than before. She closed her eyes tightly, finally freed from Lord Leicestershire's gaze, and felt her whole body tremble with a strange shudder.

"Lady Mary," she breathed, her hand touching her friend's arm. "I—I apologize. It is only that I have seen my betrothed and I—"

"Your betrothed?"

Lady Mary's eyes widened, her cheeks rapidly losing their color as she stared at Augusta with evident concern.

"You are engaged?" Lady Mary whispered as Augusta's throat tightened all the more. "When did such a thing occur?"

Augusta shook her head minutely. "It was not something of my choosing," she answered hoarsely. "My father arranged it on my behalf, without my knowledge of it. When I was present in the little Season, I was introduced to Lord Pendleton."

"Lord Pendleton?" Lady Mary exclaimed, only to close her eyes in embarrassment and drop her head.

Augusta smiled tightly. "Indeed," she said, seeing her friend's reaction and fully expecting her to be aware of the situation regarding Lord Pendleton. "He has not signed the betrothal agreement as far as I am aware, for it has not yet been returned to my father. However, given he has been in mourning for his brother, my father has not been overly eager in pursuing the matter, believing that Lord Leicestershire—as he is now—will return the papers when he is quite ready."

Lady Mary said nothing for some moments, considering all that had been said carefully and letting her eyes rove towards where Augusta had been looking towards only a few moments before.

"That is most extraordinary," she said, one hand now pressed against her heart. "And might I inquire as to whether or not you are pleased with this arrangement?"

With a wry smile, Augusta said nothing but looked at her friend with a slight lift of her eyebrow, making Lady Mary more than aware of precisely how she felt.

"I see," Lady Mary replied, her eyes still wide but seeming to fill with sympathy as she squeezed Augusta's hand, her lips thin. "I am sorry that you have had to endure such difficulties. I cannot imagine what you must have felt to be told that your marriage was all arranged without you having any awareness of such a thing beforehand!"

"It has been rather trying," Augusta admitted softly. "I have a slight hope through it all, however."

"Oh?"

Allowing herself another smile, Augusta dared a glance back towards Lord Leicestershire, only to see him still watching her. Embarrassed, she pulled her eyes away quickly, looking back to her friend. "I have a slight hope that he might decide *not* to sign the papers," she said as Lady Mary sucked in a breath. "As he is now a marquess and an heir, what if he decides that he must now choose his bride with a good deal more consideration?" Feeling a little more relaxed, no longer as anxious and as confused as she had been only a few moments before, she allowed herself a small smile. "I might be able to discover my freedom once more."

Lady Mary did not smile. Rather, her lips twisted to one side, and her brows lowered. "But would that not then mean that your father might, once again, find you another match of his choosing?" she said quietly, as though she were afraid to upset Augusta any further. "Lord Leicestershire is certainly an excellent match, Lady Augusta. He is a marquess and will have an excellent fortune. Surely he is not to be dismissed with such ease!"

Augusta allowed herself to frown, having not considered such a thing before. She did not want to be saddled with anyone of her father's choosing, instead wanting to discover a husband of her own choice. There was that choice there that, up until the previous little Season, she had always expected to have.

"I will simply speak to my father," she said airily, trying to express some sort of expectation that her father would do precisely what she asked. "He will be willing to listen to me, I am sure."

Lady Mary's expression cleared. "Well, if that is true, then I must hope that you can extricate yourself from this...if you so wish." That flickering frown remained, reminding Augusta that she was now betrothed to a marquess. A Marquess who had influence, wealth, and a high title. Was she being foolish hoping that the betrothal would come to an end? Did she truly value her own choice so much that she would throw aside something that so many others in society would pursue with everything they had?

"I..." Augusta trailed off, looking into her friend's eyes and knowing that, with Lady Mary, she had to be honest.

"I shall consider what you have said," she agreed eventually as Lady Mary's frown finally lifted completely. "You are right to state that he *is,* in fact, a marquess, and mayhap he is not a match that I should be so eager to thrust aside."

"Might I inquire as to how often you have been in his company?" Lady Mary asked, turning to stand beside Augusta so that she might look out through the ballroom a little better. "Do you know him *very* well? Does he have a difficult personality that makes your eagerness to wed him so displeasing?"

Augusta winced as a knowing look came into Lady Mary's eyes. "I confess that I have not spent any time with him at all," she admitted, "save for our introduction and, thereafter, a country dance." She lifted one shoulder in a half shrug whilst avoiding Lady Mary's gaze. "Perhaps I have been a little hasty."

Lady Mary chuckled and nodded. "Mayhap," she agreed, with a smile that lit up her expression. "He may very well be a very fine gentleman indeed, Lady Augusta, and soon, you will be considered the most fortunate of all the young ladies present in London for the Season."

As much as Augusta did not want to accept this, as much as she wanted to remain determined to make her own choice, she had to admit that Lady Mary had made some valid considerations and she ought to take some time to think through all that had been said. It was not with trepidation but with a sense of curiosity deep within her that she walked through the ballroom with Lady Mary by her side, ready to greet Lord Leicestershire again. There was a little more interest in her heart and mind now, wondering what he would say and how he would appear when he greeted her. With a deep breath, she smiled brightly as she drew near him, her heart quickening just a little as she curtsied.

"Lord Leicestershire," she said, lifting her eyes to his and noting, with a touch of alarm, that there was not even a flicker of a smile touching his lips. "Good evening. How very good to see you again."

Lord Leicestershire frowned, his brow furrowed and his eyes shadowed. "Pardon me, my lady," he said as the other gentlemen he was talking to turned their attention towards both her and Lady Mary. "But I do not recall your name. In fact," he continued, spreading his hands, "I do not think we have ever been acquainted!"

Augusta's mouth dropped open in astonishment, her eyes flaring wide and her cheeks hot with embarrassment as she saw each of the gentlemen looking at her and then glancing at each other with amusement. Lady Mary gaped at Lord Leicestershire, her hand now on Augusta's elbow.

"If you will excuse me," Augusta croaked, trying to speak with strength only for her to practically whisper. "I must..."

"You are due to dance," Lady Mary interjected, helpfully guiding Augusta away from Lord Leicestershire. "Come, Lady Augusta."

Augusta let her friend lead her from the group, feeling utter humiliation wash all over her. Keeping her head low, she allowed Lady Mary to guide her to the opposite side of the room, silently praying that no one else was watching her. Glancing from one side to the other, she heard the whispers and laughter coming from either side of her and closed her eyes tightly, fearful that the rumors and gossip were already starting. For whatever reason, Lord Leicestershire had either chosen to pretend he did not know her or truly had forgotten her, and either way, Augusta was completely humiliated.

WHAT HAPPENS next with Lady Augusta and Lord Leicestershire? Will they continue to fight or will they find a way to respect each other? Check out the rest of the story in the Kindle Store A Broken Betrothal

JOIN MY MAILING LIST

Sign up for my newsletter to stay up to date on new releases, contests, giveaways, freebies, and deals!

Free book with signup!

Monthly Giveaways! Books and Amazon gift cards! Join me on Facebook: https://www. facebook.com/rosepearsonauthor

Website: www.RosePearsonAuthor.com

Follow me on Goodreads: Author Page

You can also follow me on Bookbub! Click on the picture below – see the Follow button?

Manufactured by Amazon.ca
Bolton, ON

14687526R00143